RAW DEAL

RAW DEAL

A WESTERN MYSTERY BY

LAURAN PAINE

Golden West Press
Farmington, Maine, U.S.A.

Cover design: Christopher Wait

Published by:
Golden West Press,
an imprint of Encircle Publications

info@encirclepub.com
http://encirclepub.com

ONE

At first, there was only the steadily piling-up coldness. Then came the first light dustings of snow that lay white and clean until near high noon. Then they vanished, and the brown, moldy old earth shone through once more with its scattering of dry leaves and tawny, dead grasses.

Finally, though, there was a bitter sky overhead and a scudding wind that rushed down from the north. The cold became sharper, the earth took on a steely hue, and no one could doubt that winter had arrived.

In the line camps far out—where a cowboy or two were set to spend winter breaking trail each morning to the wood pile, to the soddy stable, or the haystack—men braided bridles, some of horsehair, some of rawhide, and beat moths out of their bearskin gauntlets and their buffalo coats.

Winter on the northern ranges could be a terror, or it could be a blessing. The problem was that no one ever knew in December what January, February, and March would bring. Even the line-camp and home-ranch conversations, while they normally contained some comments about weather, were usually very careful about long-range prognostications.

But there were always a few, like old Peter Partridge of the Yellowstone Outfit—called Puma for some reason no one seemed to know—who had a special way of getting around prognostications. Whenever old Puma Partridge was asked about the weather, he'd answer by recalling, with innumerable tart and profane embellishments, that terrible winter in '76, or that open winter of '83. Old Puma was one of those eternal procrastinators who, when asked a direct question, never gave a direct reply. It was something Puma resisted stubbornly out of principle, like admitting he might be ill, or agreeing that he was in the neighborhood of sixty years of age.

He was a bean-pole of a man and, in fact, did not look sixty. Puma thought like a man of fifteen, and he oftentimes acted like a man of twenty. But those who knew—those who had seen Puma talk *wibulta* with his fingers and arms to the few scruffy Indians who sometimes came to the Yellowstone Outfit to try their luck at begging a free meal—swore up and down that Puma had been an Army scout in the Indian wars, and before that, had been one of those old-time Mountain Men. If any of this were so, then the sixty years most folks attributed to Puma Partridge simply had to be ten, maybe even fifteen years younger than he really was.

Wild horses couldn't have dragged his age out of Puma Partridge, but the Yellowstone riders, with precious little to do in wintertime, made a game out of trying to get him to divulge that well-guarded secret, and sometimes their methods weren't much gentler than the wild horses would have been.

Old Puma had been working for the Yellowstone Outfit for seven years. He could double as camp cook, as bone-setter, as hostler, and tally-man, and he was undeniably a good hand with a horse or a rope. He was long and thin and as tough as catgut. He had a thatch of wild hair that didn't lie down even when he greased it for one of the dances and hoe-downs over at Lincoln, and his faded old eyes were eager and shrewd. He didn't miss much, and he had a memory like an Indian. In fact, old Puma was such a fixture at the Yellowstone home-ranch that when he came jogging in that leaden day with a wintry, bitter sky at his back and his old buffalo coat turned up, one of the other riders, spying him through a bunkhouse window, commented that things must be all right out with the cattle because Puma was in before dark, which ordinarily he never was.

This day, there was that peculiar rank taste to the air which presaged a snowfall. The overhead heavens were steely and shifting, first north and south, then east to west. There was a lot of static electricity in the air, too, so when Puma removed his hat in the barn to give his head a scratch, his hair sprang out every which way.

He put up his horse, removed his ragged gloves, and frowned at that forbidding sky. Then he went stumping over to the bunkhouse where a little chuck stove was merrily popping while four lounging riders played cards and drank endless gallons of coffee strong enough to float a horseshoe.

Those four scarcely heeded Puma's entrance. Only one man looked up: John Landon, who wore the only ivory-butted six-gun in that room. John was a good enough rangeman; he was inclined to swagger a little, to give short answers, and to never lack a comment about anyone or anything. John wasn't the best-liked man among those Yellowstone riders, but he was admittedly the best horse-breaker and the best rider among them. He was respected, but the others didn't really warm up to him.

John said with a sneer, "Hey, Puma, someday a hunter'll spot you in that buffler coat an' shoot you for camp meat."

No one laughed, but the foreman, good-natured and quietly efficient Vern Patton, tossed down his cards and twisted to look over where Puma stood with his back to them all as he shrugged out of his coat.

"How were the cattle?" Vern asked.

"Fine," Puma said, "the ones I seen," and hung his coat upon the upright post at the foot of his wall bunk. "Man, but she's gettin' cold out there," he threw in as he turned and dropped down upon the edge of his bunk. He saw all those heads slowly come around and fasten upon him with wide-popped eyes. As though he didn't observe this sudden and astonished attention, he said, "Goin' to storm tonight, sure as I'm a foot tall."

Vern Patton kicked fully around on the bench. The others put down their cards. Even John Landon's mouth was agape.

Vern said very quietly, "Puma, you been shot."

For a moment, old Puma simply looked at those astonished, heat-flushed faces before he lowered his head and sat there gravely considering the big, sticky stain of crimson below his left shoulder.

"So I have," he agreed. He looked up again, ran a glance over towards the cookstove, and said, "Say, who's supposed to get supper tonight?"

Vern Patton stood up. "All right," Vern said. "You've made your point. You're too tough for bullets to hurt." Vern walked over close and halted. He bent from the middle to squint at the bloodstain. The bunkhouse was lit by one smoked-up, coal-oil lamp, which no one ever thought to clean, so visibility was never very good, and today, with the yard outside turning steadily blacker as afternoon advanced, there was no other light to see by.

Vern straightened back up, put his big hands upon his hips, and gazed both critically and interestedly at Puma.

"What happened?" he asked.

The others came over to gaze at that gunshot wound. John Landon made one of his irrefutable but unsubstantiated pronouncements: "Winchester slug done that. No six-gun."

Puma looked up and slowly nodded. He did not cherish the fact that John was correct, but old Puma could not very well refute the obvious either.

"Yup, Winchester," he grunted.

"Out with it," ordered the range boss, his normally good-natured features turning hard. "Who did it and where did it happen?"

"Tore my consarned coat, too," muttered Puma, reaching out to finger that mangy old buffalo garment where it hung. "Wish I could've nailed him. As it turned out, though, there wasn't nothin' to shoot at."

Vern growled, "Doggone it, Puma, I asked—"

"Keep your shirt on," said Puma irritably. "I'm tellin' you." He paused to make certain of his audience, then spoke on.

"I was east of the Devil's Postpile over in them cussed rocks where sometimes critters bunch up when they smell a storm comin'. It was blustery, and I turned up my coat collar. Still had my arms raised up when someone fired a carbine. I heard it plain as day, even with that danged wind a-blowin'. It was like bein' stung by a hornet as big as a mule."

"Knock you off?" asked Drew Ruddabaugh, youngest of the Yellowstone riders.

"Hmph!" snorted Puma. "How could it knock me off? Was only one bullet, wasn't it? Well, anyway, I never seen that feller at all. Never even seen his horse, but he had to be in them boulders somewheres around."

"What'd you do?"

"Why, I turned that jug-headed horse around, and I rode on home. 'Bout a mile off, though, I opened my coat to see how bad it was. It wasn't hurtin' much then, just sort of numb-like. Then I come on back, and here I am."

Vern Patton ran a hand over his bristly jaw and stared at old Puma. Finally, lowering that hand, he said, "John, you 'n' Drew heat up some water and take care of that for him."

"Ahhh," old Puma articulated, "I don't need no help patchin' this thing up."

"You let them fix that," snapped Vern, a little exasperated at the old rider's persistent belittling of his injury. "You're tough, Puma, an' you've had worse hurts, I know. Lord knows you've told us often enough about 'em. But all the same, it's seventeen miles to Lincoln, and if you get infection in that thing, or come down with a fever," Vern solemnly wagged his head. "This time of the year, it's awful hard breakin' that frozen earth for diggin' graves."

Drew and the cowboy beside him, dark and bulky Martin Caine, made little smiles. For Martin, this was quite a concession—he rarely smiled about anything. He was a dark, handsome man with all the swarthiness of Latin blood. He'd only been with the Yellowstone Outfit this past year, and so, was the newest rider among them.

Landon poured a pan full of water, put it upon the little chuck-stove, and stood over there running what Puma had told them through his mind. Eventually, he turned and said, with a strong look of doubt, of wonderment, "Why in hell would anyone shoot a man who's just ridin' along? And if you wanted to shoot a man, would you let him turn and ride off after just one shot?"

Martin Caine sauntered back to the battered bunkhouse table, straddled a bench, and gazed over at John. "I'll tell you why you'd do it like that," he said quietly. "Because you was in the rocks and didn't want no one comin' onto you. And you didn't really want to kill old Puma, you just wanted to scare him off."

"Ahhh," scoffed John. "But a shot over his head would've done that, Martin. I believe that feller was deliberately tryin' to kill him."

Vern Patton walked over where his sheepskin hung, shrugged into the thing, then scooped up his hat, dropped it atop his head, and crossed over to the bunkhouse door.

"One thing's sure," he stated emphatically. "Whoever he is, he's got no business on Yellowstone range. As for ridin' around takin' pot-shots at folks—I've got a spankin' new hard-twist lariat made to measure for his cussed throat. And I also happen to know where there's just the right size oak tree to string him up from."

Vern looked broodily at Puma, as Drew Ruddabaugh was trying to help the injured man shed his shirt and lower his high-buttoned underwear-tops. Drew wasn't getting much cooperation. Puma growled at him to 'go suck eggs,' said he didn't need any runny-nosed youngster to help *him* just because he had a cussed bullet hole through his shoulder.

Vern said sternly, "You let them take care of that thing, Puma, doggone your ornery old hide. I'm goin' over to the main house and tell Mister Poirer about this. Cut out that faunchin' around, Puma. Sit still an' let 'im fix that hole."

Puma sat still, but he looked sullenly indignant.

Vern opened the door. A frigid blast of wind sprang inside, making the lamp dip and gyrate frantically. Then he closed the door behind him, hunched up, and struck out across the yard.

TWO

Abel Poirer was a large man. He was tall and raw-boned and loose-moving. He was also gray and steady-eyed. He had an air to him of solid accomplishment, as well he might have. He'd been in Wyoming a quarter century, and every day of that time, he'd worked towards putting together one of the largest, most prosperous cow-calf outfits for two hundred miles in any direction.

He was not a simple man, nor was he a man easy to know or associate with. He ruled his domain like an iron duke straight out of the Middle Ages. He seldom had much to say to his riders, transacted ranch business through the range boss Vern Patton, and did not, as many owners did, go out with the roundup wagon in the spring or in the fall.

He seemed to make a special point of never arriving in the town of Lincoln, seventeen miles east of his Yellowstone Outfit, without an escort of his Yellowstone men. In fact, Abel Poirer was that aloof, iron-like type of man that everyone mightily respected but no one ever knew well enough personally to be friendly towards.

And nothing seemingly ever threw him. Even that blustery, gusty night with the lead-belly sky a hundred feet overhead scudding west with its promise of snow, when Vern beat upon the main-house door and Abel Poirer's wife admitted him. She was instantly solicitous for Vern's comfort because that was her nature. She told him to go stand by the stove while she went after some hot coffee for him. But Abel simply stood there awesomely tall and rangy, his thatch of gray hair carefully combed back, his unwavering eyes upon the range boss, and waited for Vern to say whatever had brought him.

Vern did; he related all he knew about the shooting of Puma Partridge, gratefully accepted the coffee when Mrs. Poirer brought it, and he stood there uncomfortably, waiting for Abel Poirer to speak. Abel had that unique propensity for deep silences which made people, even the ones like Vern who'd known him several years, distinctly uncomfortable in his presence.

Finally, he said, "Knowing Puma, I'm wondering if it wasn't something personal."

Vern shook his head. "I doubt it," he said in quiet disagreement. "He didn't know that man was there or he'd never have been caught flat-footed like that, Mister Poirer."

"On the other hand," Poirer persisted, "if the other

man had known Puma might be out looking for him, he probably wouldn't have waited for Puma to see him first, either."

Vern shrugged. He didn't accept any of this, but he wasn't going to provoke an argument over something neither of them actually knew anything about. Eventually, he said, "I'll take the crew out in the morning and see what we can find."

Poirer had evidently been expecting this, for he made a little indifferent gesture and said, "By morning, there'll be six inches of snow on the ground. You won't find the man or his tracks."

Poirer faintly frowned. He paced over by the stove, whirled, clasped both hands behind him, and gazed from his wife, who was sitting quietly with some knitting, on over to Vern.

"He'd probably be a stranger, Vern. Possibly some outlaw with man-hunters on his trail. He wouldn't be a local man, I don't think, because everyone hereabouts knows this is Yellowstone range, and we don't encourage trespassers."

"Maybe," murmured Vern, putting aside his emptied coffee cup. "And maybe it was rustlers."

"Poor night for stealing beef, Vern. You can't see fifty feet ahead of you."

"Well, whoever he was, he sure meant business, Mister Poirer."

"You go back to the bunkhouse and find out whether Puma has any idea why that man shot at him. Find out who he's argued with lately over in town, or any other place for that matter. You know how he gets sometimes, Vern, argumentative and hard to live with."

Vern started for the door, stopped suddenly, and put his head a little to one side. Out in the gusty night, a man's sharp outcry was borne over the yard. It was a high cry difficult to separate from the wind's own keening moans.

Abel Poirer and his wife also heard that sound. She sat straight up in her chair. Abel crossed over beside Vern in four big strides and threw out his arm, restraining the younger man. Just for that short moment, Abel Poirer was as he'd been two decades earlier: wary and alert and alive to possible peril.

"Not out the front door," he barked at his range boss. "Never with the light behind you. Go out through the kitchen, Vern, and stay to the side of the house. Be careful."

As Vern obediently reversed his course, Abel Poirer went to the polished lamps and one by one blew them out until his parlor was plunged in utter darkness.

"Nettie," he said quietly to Mrs. Poirer. "You stay down and be still."

Abel was heading for the front door when a fisted hand struck that panel from out in the night with a quick, rough urgency.

"Who is it?" challenged Abel Poirer, reaching under his Prince Albert coat to draw forth a little under-and-over .41 caliber Derringer pistol. "Who is it and what do you want?"

"It's John Landon, Mister Poirer. Is Vern in there?"

Abel moved up, grasped the latch, flung back the door, and raised his pistol, at the same time turning sideways. "Come in here," he snapped at the bulky man-shape out in the windy, bitter night.

Landon entered. He was hatless and had his sheepskin rider's coat folded back to expose the ivory butt of his hip-holstered six-gun.

"Close the door," ordered Poirer. Then he said, lowering his little hide-out pistol and squaring around in the dark, "What is it, John?"

"I was looking for Vern. A horse come into the yard. Young Ruddabaugh was outside an' saw it. He went over, caught the critter, led it into the barn, and lit a lamp to see whose critter it was. Mister Poirer, it's not one of our animals, an' it's got a saddle on it. There's blood on the saddle."

"Nettie," said Poirer to his wife back there in the darkness. "Light the lamps again." To John Landon he said, "A loose horse?"

"Yessir. The reins are busted off short like it was runnin' maybe, an' stepped on 'em."

"Did any of you recognize the outfit?"

"No. We all went out to the barn an' looked it over, but none of us ever saw it before."

"Did Puma go look, too?"

"Well, no, he's not feelin' so good right about now."

Nettie Poirer lit the lamps one by one. Outside, someone gently knocked, and Poirer opened the door to admit Vern Patton. "Tell Vern," said Abel, "I'll get my coat and go with you."

As soon as her husband was out of the room, Nettie Poirer turned, watched those two coated, stalwart men speaking softly back and forth over by the door, and interrupted them to ask a question.

"Boys, if someone's been hurt and is lying out on the range somewhere—is there a chance of finding him before the snow comes?"

Vern and John exchanged a look. There was a chance of finding him, whoever he was, but it was an almighty slim chance.

Vern said carefully, "We would try, ma'am. But there's no tellin' where he might be."

"Did Puma tell you where that shot was fired at him?"

"Yes'm. Over by the Devil's Postpile, in among the boulders over there."

"Well then, I think I'd start looking over there," said dark and tiny Nettie Poirer.

Vern and John exchanged another look. This was a sound suggestion, they both knew it, and afterward, they looked back at Abel Poirer's wife a little wondering and a little respectful.

"Yes'm."

Abel returned. He had his gun-belt and his sheepskin coat. He also had his battered old black hat, the one he invariably wore on the range. He didn't seem so distant, so aloof and granite-like now; he seemed more like a working cowman. He threw a little nod at his wife, jerked his head, and passed on out into the stormy night.

The three of them had to brace forward into the punishing wind, but they had the onward lodestar of lamplight to guide them across to the big log barn. Once inside, over there, the wind no longer tore at them, but its rough scrabblings under barn-eaves made a fitful moaning.

Abel Poirer walked straight up where Drew Ruddabaugh and Martin Caine were standing with a stocky sorrel gelding. Abel ignored those two as he slowly stepped around that animal, noting that it had been running, noting also that unmistakable dark, sticky crimson upon the saddle leather.

Vern did the same thing; he walked out and around the sorrel making his assessments, and ultimately he said, "Texas A-fork saddle, double Navajo blanket, California silver-mounted spade bit with Santa Barbara cheekpieces. Whoever he is, he's sure no Wyoming man."

"Southwest," Martin Caine assented, with a grave nod of his head. "An' I'd guess the carbine there in its scabbard—"

Martin never got that sentence completed. Abel Poirer stepped up, yanked out that gun, levered it once, and they all turned silent, turned watchful, as an empty casing jumped out and fell to the earthen floor where it wickedly shone under yellow lamp-light.

Abel raised smoky eyes to Vern. "Find the man who owns this gun, and I think you'll also have the man who shot Puma."

Abel closed the carbine's breech with a harsh, metallic meshing of steel parts, shoved the gun back into its saddle-boot, and jerked his head.

"Off-saddle him. Put him in a stall and fork him some feed."

He specified no one in particular for this chore, but Drew and Martin moved up to obey. Vern and John Landon, standing there solemnly watching, switched their attention only when Abel Poirer crossed over to them.

"Let's get mounted," he said to his range boss. "Whoever he is, if he isn't dead by now, he will be by morning. I don't know whether he's worth saving or not, but we've got to find out."

Vern murmured, "Maybe we'd better go over by Devil's Postpile for our first look. That's where someone plugged Puma."

Poirer brusquely nodded and strode away after a horse. The others also rigged out stabled animals. The last man to swing up over leather was Martin Caine. He took time out to button his sheepskin all the way up under his chin, but he was careful to make sure the lower portion of his coat was still securely tucked clear of his ivory-butted six-gun.

The five of them rode on out into the yard, hesitated for a second as that buffeting, wild wind struck them, then pushed on northeasterly with Abel Poirer up in the lead.

For a half hour, there was only that freezing wind to contend with, but beyond that, there were also stinging little icy particles that beat into their faces, forcing each man to crouch lower into his coat and seek protection from that invisible, whipping first snowfall by lowering his head and tucking his chin below a coat collar.

The horses, unable to turn tail to this punishment, constantly tossed their heads, blew their noses, and tried to turn back. All this earned them was some warm profanity which the wind whipped rearward as soon as it was uttered.

There was no lull to this storm, but neither was there any consistent direction to its force and tumult. One moment, the wind would whoop down from the frozen north. The next moment, it would shift entirely and come howling up out of the south. It was as though the five of them were struggling along through the very center, the very vortex, of this storm.

That stinging snowfall intensified too, each flake frozen hard and with innumerable little sharp daggers to it, which unmercifully stung congealing flesh.

Abel Poirer bored right on through as though he were made of impervious iron. Behind him, the others rode bunched up and bent forward, scarcely heeding their route or progress. The cold was not entirely turned aside by their coats, but at least movement kept their upper bodies from chilling. This was not the case with their exposed legs, though. By the time they were close enough to make out that immense boulder-field, which was called the Devil's Postpile, not a one of them could feel anything in their feet and legs but a solid, frozen lumpiness.

Abel swung down. This brought the others to a sluggish halt. Vern and John Landon also dismounted. These three tossed their reins up to Drew and Martin, then went stumbling ahead over rock-like frozen sod.

When they got behind the first huge stone, which was as tall and thick as a large house, there was a sudden, blessed release from fighting the wind. They remained there for a moment, breathing hard, then started onward again.

Abel was slightly ahead. Vern saw him stumble, go down, and catch himself clumsily. Vern also heard

Abel's curse as he did this. He moved up to give Abel a hand. So did John Landon. Afterwards, the three of them stood like granite staring down at what Abel had stumbled over. It was the sprawled, stiff, crumpled body of a man.

Abel turned and bawled for the others, his voice a bull-bass in the screeching night. Drew and Martin got stiffly down, rolled the prone man over, peered closely at his face, and shook their heads at one another. Whoever he was, neither of them had ever seen him before.

THREE

Getting that stranger back to the home ranch was no simple chore. Since he had no horse, he had to be put up behind Drew Ruddabaugh with Martin Caine and John Landon on either side to steady the man. He was as limp and lifeless-seeming as a man could be, but fortunately, at least for this unpleasant trip, the cold had turned him stiff enough for the others to hold.

Again, Abel led out. He pushed along with the unerring instinctiveness of a quarter century straight for his barn. He didn't miss that building by one foot, although for the last thousand yards it was snowing so hard none of them could see any further than ten feet ahead.

Now, though, that whipping wind died down to fitful bursts, and replacing all the earlier howling was a crushing silence.

Snow fell in a smooth-flowing way without seeming to hurry any or to slow any, just a constant white drift so thick a man's hat brim built up with the stuff until he gradually became conscious of its dry weight and knocked it off.

They were white-mantled when they finally rode on into the barn, got down, and struck that snow off themselves. They got the sodden wreck of humanity down gingerly from behind Drew and, for the length of time required to care for their animals, left him lying there upon the earthen floor.

They moved him on to the bunkhouse with Abel going ahead to open the door, turn up the lamp, and indicate an empty, unoccupied bunk as the others brought the stranger in and put him down.

Old Puma craned his neck from where he lay under two grimy Hudson's Bay wool blankets across the room in his bunk and stared but said nothing.

The others stepped back to make room for Poirer. He bent over the stranger, removed the man's hat, and proceeded to unbutton his sheepskin rider's coat. It was so utterly hushed in the roundabout night that the little guttering sounds of the lamp could be distinctly heard as Abel opened the stranger's clothing, exposing two purple punctures, one through the fleshy topmost part of the left arm, the other lower, through the stranger's chest.

John Landon spoke out with authority in his voice, as though he knew about these things. "Clean shots, both of 'em. Whoever got him wasn't too far off when they fired."

But Vern, pursuing a different train of thought, said perplexedly, "Yeah, but who? He fell right where we found him, so who was out there tonight to shoot him, and why were they out there?"

Abel straightened back, gazed at those two bullet wounds, and said without looking around, "We'll need hot water and some bandagin' cloth. Lucky for this man, he got shot close up. Both the slugs kept right on going."

"Looks like he's lost a sight of blood," croaked Puma from across the room, "Who the hell is he, anyway?"

"Just guessing," said Abel in reply to Puma, "I'd say he's the man who shot you. I'd also say that you happened onto him no more than a minute or two after he was shot." Abel turned to gaze over at Puma. "Didn't you hear anything? Two gunshots make a lot of noise."

"That wind was blowin' ever' which way, Mister Poirer," exclaimed Puma defensively, as though he thought he was being accused of some dereliction. "I didn't hear nothin' that put me in mind of gunshots. All I heard was the cussed wind."

"But you heard the shot when he fired at you."

Puma frowned and reluctantly nodded. He didn't say anything, though, because he didn't know what he should say. He simply shrugged, winced when he did this, and looked at those smoothed-out considering laces around him.

John went to the stove to boil water for the unconscious stranger exactly as he'd done for Puma somewhat earlier. Abel turned back to thoughtfully consider the unconscious man briefly before saying, "Vern, go fetch his saddlebags in here. They ought to tell us who he is. What he was doing out there tonight."

Vern departed.

Drew Ruddabaugh stepped in closer, where he stared at the stranger. Martin Caine also moved up, but those two were only curious; neither showed by expression or gesture that they knew the wounded man.

Vern returned, kicked snow off his boots at the door, hiked on inside, and flung down a pair of saddlebags upon the bunkhouse table.

Everyone except old Puma crowded up as Abel unbuckled the bags, upended them, and considered the contents which spilled out. There was the usual change of attire riders carried, a box of .45 slugs, and a box of .25-.35 Winchester carbine slugs for a Model '94, but what Abel was specifically seeking was not there at all—the little bundle of treasured letters riders generally carried, the link with a nostalgic past members of a foot-loose fraternity almost invariably cherished and never discarded.

Abel showed disappointment in his expression until John Landon, spying something, reached down, shook out a long white envelope, and held it up for Abel to take.

There was no name on this envelope, and its cleanliness indicated that the stranger had only recently come by it. Abel opened the envelope, extracted what appeared to be a legal document of some kind, shook this long, crisp paper out, and began reading it.

No one said anything. They stood there expectantly until John, drawn away by water boiling over on the chuck-stove, turned and walked off. The sound of Landon's spurred boots seemed to jar Abel Poirer back to an awareness of the others. He lowered that paper, looked at his riders, and drew his mouth downward.

"This is a land patent," Abel said coldly. "Our stranger here has managed to homestead a hundred and sixty acres bordering Assiniboin Creek over near the Postpile and running arrow-straight for a half mile out into the heart of Yellowstone range."

Abel put the paper down. They all turned and looked over at the stranger. If there had been any solicitous compassion in their faces before, there was none now.

"A stinkin' damned squatter," croaked old Puma. "An' the son of a gun shot me 'cause I come onto him stakin' out his lousy claim. Boys, he'p me up out'n here. I aim to pay that feller back for—"

"Never mind," said Abel in that same crisp, cold tone. "Someone paid him back even before he shot you, Puma." Abel crossed over, looked down, and for a long while, he said no more.

John Landon brought the water, the bandages, and a battered tin of the range riders' cure-all—goose grease. He perched on the side of the bunk and began working over the injured man.

Martin Caine dropped down at the table, began working up a brown-paper cigarette, and from time to time put his black, hard stare over at the wounded man. Vern and Drew also sat down. Abel didn't; he remained standing at the foot of the bunk watching John work.

He said, "Why did someone shoot this squatter? Who else was out there in the storm?"

Vern, who'd wondered these same things earlier, bobbed his head up and down, saying, "Yeah, what was the other feller doin' out there? I can imagine a dozen places I'd rather be on a night like this one. Ridin' around in the dark an' the wind sure isn't one of 'em."

The stranger groaned, and every man in the bunkhouse straightened towards him. It had taken a long time for the good warmth of that square log room to relax the stranger, to cook the chill out of his flesh and his bones, but when that had finally happened, it had also melted out the numbness, and now the man was feeling pain. He rolled his head and weakly writhed. John Landon growled at him to be quiet, to lie still. Landon's voice seemed to trigger something in the stranger's brain because he suddenly became quite still and opened his eyes to look carefully around.

It could not have been a pleasant sight he first beheld, all those tough, bitter faces gazing accusingly at him as the Yellowstone men glowered. There was nothing within the law to their minds worse than a squatter; squatters came to homestead land that the big outfits had been using for decades. They put up fences, ploughed under the good grassland, and they had a reputation for rustling beef from the big outfits when conditions worsened for them, as conditions invariably did, because it was just not possible to make a living on one hundred and sixty acres of homestead land.

John Landon worked for a while with the stranger's gray eyes upon him, then John straightened back, turned, and frowned. That steady staring annoyed him.

Abel said, "Stranger, what's your name?"

The stranger swiveled his glance, considered big Abel Poirer, and said nothing.

Landon's scowl darkened. "Answer up," he growled. "Mister Poirer just asked you a question."

This time, those gray eyes jumped to Landon's face and lingered there before making a very careful roundabout trip of all the other faces in that room. But still, the wounded man said nothing.

Old Puma said, "Maybe he can't talk. Maybe one of them bullets done busted somethin' inside him an' now he—"

"He can talk," said Abel, looking flintily downward. "One of you boys fetch him a cup of hot coffee."

Drew Ruddabaugh rose up to obey this order, and Martin Caine also stood. Martin slouched over, leaned upon the wall, and stonily stared. The stranger saw Martin, returned Caine's stare for a long while, then heavily and tiredly dropped his lids.

John Landon went back to his doctoring. He finished the job, put aside his basin of pink water, dried his hands upon the stranger's shirt, and felt around for his tobacco sack.

"We'll get nothing out of him for a while," he said to Abel. "I'd say it was the loss of blood. Lord knows his shirt and coat are soaked. They lose enough blood an' they get drowsy."

This appeared to sum things up adequately, at least for the time being. Martin crossed to his own bunk, began shaking out of his coat, and tossed his hat down. Even old Puma dropped back down under his blankets. "Someone toss another chunk of wood in the stove," he murmured, turned up onto his uninjured side, and composed himself for sleep.

Abel Poirer stood with his hands clasped behind him, staring at the stranger. When Drew brought the coffee, though, Abel shook his head.

"Let him rest," he said. "He looks like he needs sleep and warmth now more than food."

John stood up, took the basin away, and afterwards went over to Vern at the stove. He said quietly, "I got a hunch we've only got the small part of something here. He didn't shoot himself, an' if there are others sneakin' around on Yellowstone range, I got a feelin' we've only just begun to turn up something."

Abel left them, and Vern went over to drop the drawbar into place across the bunkhouse door. He stepped over to a little front window and peered out.

It was still snowing, the outside yard looked ghostly, and snow had silently piled up in each corner of the window pane. There wasn't much of a moon out this night; the starshine lay softly over everything, brightening that beautiful, mysterious, and fiercely cold outside world.

"If he'd been out there another couple of hours," Vern mused aloud, "he'd have been frozen stiff."

Drew was kicking off his boots. He looked over and said, "I wouldn't even wish that on a squatter."

Vern turned, looked at his men, each of them in the process of shedding his outside attire, walked over, and picked up that legal document and held it up to the smoking lamp for a moment before tossing it down again.

"Odd," he said. "This thing doesn't have anyone's name on it. I thought legal papers always had to have someone's name on 'em."

John Landon shrugged. His attitude clearly said he knew nothing of legal processes and cared less. Martin Caine seemed uninterested, too. Drew Ruddabaugh scratched his head. "Maybe," he suggested, "these squatters fill in their names after they locate their land. Or somethin' like that."

Vern nodded over this. It seemed logical, in a way, but he'd never have personally done anything like that.

The wind was starting up again outside. It rattled one of the two front windows, then swung off and rushed upwards and southwards over the roof.

Vern listened a moment, passed on over to the chuck-stove, selected a knotty piece of pine, and chucked it into the fire-box. He looked around to be sure the others were bedded down, then, being the last man stirring, he blew out the lamp and groped over to his own bunk.

Sometimes, he idly thought as he shrugged out of his coat and upper attire, things went like this: a man was prepared to comfortably ride out a stormy night at poker in the bunkhouse with the stove popping, and then fate intervened, yanked the man away from all his comforts, and set him to bucking a wild wind to locate and fetch back a total stranger with gunshot wounds in his carcass.

Vern got under his blankets, lowered his head, and began a brand new line of speculation. What would become of big cow outfits like the Yellowstone in, say, another five, six years, if these clod-hopping nesters kept taking up the rangelands? More to the point, what would become of men like himself who only knew this one kind of existence?

He didn't like what his logic told him, so he grunted up onto his side, closed his eyes, thought of a fierce curse for men like the stranger, and went to sleep.

FOUR

That ensuing day and fifteen more like it passed before the stranger was strong enough to sit up. In all that time, he'd said no more than twenty words, and he never did tell them what his name was.

In a sense, too, he was directly responsible for Puma's quick recovery. "I couldn't stay in there one more blessed day," Puma growled at Vern the afternoon of the sixteenth day when the riders returned from checking on Yellowstone cattle, "without stranglin' that feller. He lies there staring at the ceilin' an' never openin' his blessed mouth. It's like talkin' to yourself."

Vern nodded as he and the others put up their horses. It had been the same with each of them. When they tried being friendly, the stranger gave them his cold-steel stare. When they were hostile, he gazed at each of them as though to indelibly imprint their hostile faces in his mind. When they shook that homestead patent under his nose, he was like granite. In the end, they accepted his presence much as they'd have acknowledged the existence of a big stone they couldn't get rid of, didn't like, and had to walk around. They fed him, cared for his horse, looked after his simple wants as they'd have done for even a bronco-buck Indian who was injured, but they didn't like him and didn't want him around.

On the twentieth day, Abel came across through a raw wind from the main-house with a bundle of food Nettie had made up. She'd only visited the stranger once, had been repulsed, and had never come again.

Abel entered the bunkhouse, threw a careless look at his silent men, crossed to where the stranger sat, fully clothed upon the edge of his bunk, and tossed down Nettie's bundle. Abel said nothing. It was against range etiquette to ever tell a man he'd overstayed his welcome, but, like handing him a bundle of food, there were ways of getting that idea across to him.

The stranger considered the bundle, considered big, rawboned Abel, got up and crossed to the bunkhouse table. He had his back to Abel and the others when he took up his blood-stiff sheepskin, rummaged inside its lining, drew forth four gold coins, and dropped them. Puma saw that gold money first and was startled at the sight. Gold coins were not only rare in Wyoming, but only people of substance ever possessed them.

"That ought to settle things," the stranger said, putting his wintry stare upon Abel. "A hundred dollars in gold."

Vern flushed and stepped around where he could see

the man's face. Vern was indignant. "A hundred dollars more'n pays for what we've done for you, mister, if you're figurin' the value of the food and whatnot. But money never pays for savin' a life, does it?"

Puma, who'd been badgering the stranger ever since they'd been confined together, chirped up. He called the stranger by the name he'd given him weeks before, and it fit, not just because none of them knew any other name for him, but because he obviously was that kind of a man.

Puma said, "Loner, what kind of a man ain't got the decency in him to say just one 'thank you'?"

Abel interrupted here. He said gruffly, "Forget it. It's done. I don't think his life's worth a hundred dollars anyway. No squatter's life is worth that."

The loner stood gazing at those four coins. He was a solid, powerful man who tapered from thick shoulders to a rider's narrow waist. He wore his gun, not like all the others in that room, not low on his right thigh, but belted high and on the left side of his trouser-belt, the butt reversed for a right-hand draw. This method of using a six-gun was called the 'border cross,' and in the hands of those experienced in it, it was very lethal.

There were certain tell-tale, obvious things about this stranger the others had not overlooked; they said mutely yet quite plainly that the loner was capable, shrewd, and possibly dangerous. He'd be a top-hand on the trail, around the marking-fires, in strange or hostile towns. Even John Landon, with his ivory-butted .45 and his know-it-all attitude, treated the loner with unmistakable and unconscious deference. Even Abel Poirer treated the man almost as an equal.

It was Abel who quietly said, "If I were you, Loner, and I figured to put up a shack on that homestead of yours, I'd develop an eye in the back of my head."

This seemed to spark something in the stranger's mind, for he turned and gazed consideringly over at big Abel. "Homestead hell," he said. "I didn't come here to squat."

"No? Then what about that land patent?"

The loner rummaged a coat pocket, brought out that crisp envelope, and tossed it across at Abel's feet. "It's yours," he said coldly, "for nothing."

Abel looked down at the envelope, up at the loner, then around at the other watching men in the bunkhouse. He clearly did not understand what was being done here.

The loner said, "All you got to do is fill in your name on it, make the required improvements, and at the end of the proving-up time, according to the law, that land is yours. That satisfy you, Poirer?"

Abel still said nothing. Not for a long time, but ultimately he reached up, pushed back his hat, and said, "You owe me nothing. I'd have done as much for a hurt dog."

"Maybe, but Vern and the others think I'm ungrateful for the saving of my life. I'm not ungrateful, I'm just not the 'thank you' type. I pay my way, I always have, and I always will."

The loner picked up his saddlebags, slung them over his right shoulder, put on his hat, and walked as far as the bunkhouse door before turning to cast a final, frosty look at those silent, watching Yellowstone men.

"I make my livin' that way," he told those blank-faced men. "You won't approve, but that doesn't mean anything to me."

"What way?" asked Abel.

"You want to keep your range, don't you?" retorted the loner. "All right. I fix it so's the big outfits don't get broken up. I hang around the federal land offices, and when someone takes out homestead papers, I offer 'em anywhere from ten to a hundred dollars for their claim. Then I sell that land to the nearest big cow outfit." The loner nodded down where that envelope still lay at Abel's feet. "That'll explain why there's no name on the papers. I have the seller make 'em out that way on purpose. Now do you understand?"

"Just a second," said Vern Patton. "Is that legal?"

The loner gazed frostily at Vern. "Beats robbing stages all to hell, cowboy. If you've got doubts, there's a town about fifteen miles from here. Go ask some law-book feller over there."

Abel said, "Were you in that town, Loner?"

"I was in it, Poirer. I stayed there two days until I got the lay of the land. I'm heading back for it now, too. Ordinarily, I wouldn't stay here—in my business, you peddle your land and be on your way to the next place. But there's some unfinished business hereabouts, so maybe I'll be around for a few more days."

"More land to sell?" asked Abel.

The loner shook his head. "I've got more land, but that's not what I want to work on now. I want the man who shot me."

John Landon said dryly, "Good luck. I'm almighty curious about that too. I'm kind of curious about something else, too. Why would a man try an' stake out his homestead on a wild, stormy night when he couldn't see his hand in front of his face, like you were doing."

The stranger gazed at Landon. He seemed to have some special thoughts about John. He said, "I wasn't stakin' out anything. I knew where the land was from maps. And I wasn't out there after nightfall, cowboy, I was out there in broad daylight. I located the land, looked it over, and was fixin' to head back when the storm started thickening. That was when someone shot me."

"Yeah," exclaimed old Puma Partridge, "and that's also when you shot me, too, mister."

The loner nodded. "That was a mistake," he said. "I was about half out of my head. I guess I'd been knocked out. Anyway, when I rolled over, I saw you sittin' out there on your horse, figured you were goin' to finish me off, and I protected myself." The loner fished around inside his coat, brought forth a fifty-dollar gold piece, which he flipped over at Puma. The old cowboy caught it, held the coin up where he could determine its worth, and his brows went swiftly crawling upwards like two caterpillars. All the antagonism left old Puma's face in a twinkling. Fifty dollars was once and a half what he made each month working for Abel Poirer.

"No hard feelings," said the loner.

Puma made a grin so broad it threatened to split his face wide open. "None at all," he chortled. "Come down and have another shot at me sometime."

"I just might do that," said the loner. He was not smiling.

Abel caught the meaning here ahead of the others. "Do you think one of my men shot you?" he asked.

The loner shrugged. "None of them have denied it. None of them liked the idea of having what they thought was a squatter amongst 'em. I'm asking no questions, Poirer, but I'll find out who did that."

Vern's eyes turned cold, his expression hardened. "Mister, if any of us had wanted to shoot you, we wouldn't have afterwards worked hard at saving your lousy life."

"Yeah," murmured the loner. "That's what's been

stickin' in my head, Patton. That's all that's kept me from takin' you boys apart."

John Landon's head came up at this bold statement, but John only stared, not saying anything. Neither did the loner; he just returned John's hard look, then he lifted the door latch and walked out of the bunkhouse.

Abel stood for a long moment in deep thought. Around him, the others spoke back and forth. All but old Puma, who bit that gold coin, skeptically held it up to the light, hefted it for honest weight, and finally, delightedly, resigned himself to the fact that it was neither hollow nor counterfeit.

Abel walked out of the bunkhouse, still looking pensive. He crossed through dirty snow and frozen puddles to the barn where the stranger was rigging out his fat and sassy horse. The loner threw Abel a look, then went on with what he was doing as though Abel didn't exist.

For a while, Abel only watched the sure, experienced manner in which the loner worked. He leaned against a stall partition, carefully appraising the other man. There was something moving in the hard depths of Abel's eyes that was normally absent when Abel gazed upon other men. It was a mixture of respect, wonderment, and something akin to an expression of equality. Abel was brusque, and he was cold and normally aloof, but he was an excellent judge of men. This stranger was not in his view a common man at all, and Abel was more than just curious.

"Tell me something," he ultimately said. "Have you been at this business of yours very long?"

"Long enough," said the loner.

"You make money at it?"

The loner turned. He had his horse ready. He stood there with one split rein in his hand, frostily eyeing Abel Poirer. "Come to the point," he said. "You're not really interested in whether or not I've made money at this."

Abel would ordinarily have bristled; no one used that rough tone to him. But now, surprisingly enough, he didn't show antagonism at all. It was as though he'd come to accept the shortness and bluntness of the other man.

"The point," he said evenly, "is simple enough, Loner. I've been wondering if you have any more of those patents."

"I have."

"I see. I figured you might have. And are they all for Yellowstone range?"

"They're all for *open* range, Poirer. You don't own this Yellowstone range, you only use it. That's what the Homestead Law is all about. It makes available to anyone who's simple-minded enough to think they can make a livin' in this country, free land for homesteading."

"But those other papers you have—they're for Yellowstone range, aren't they?"

"They are. What of it? You want to try and get them by force?"

Abel pushed up off the partition at his back. He shook his head. "Loner, that chip on your shoulder is pretty heavy, isn't it? What makes a man with your brains so bitter towards all other men?"

The stranger's wintry stare darkened. He said very softly, "Poirer, I'll be at the hotel in Lincoln for the next three, four days. If you want to talk business, look me up. If you want to stick your big nose where it's got no business, you might get it broken."

The loner stepped up over leather, eased down, and shortened his reins. Outside, there was a dazzlingly bright sun shining. The air was cold enough to make the breath of man and beast steamy-white, and a skiff of fresh snow lay underfoot. Farther out, banked snow still lay from that first storm of the year, which had cowed the land the night the loner was found shot and brought to Poirer's Yellowstone outfit.

"I'll look you up," murmured Abel to the mounted man. "I'm curious too about who shot you on my land and why they did it. I'm curious about a lot of things, Loner." Abel walked along as the stranger reined out of the barn. He halted beyond the doorway, gazing upwards at the loner.

"Answer one more question for me, Loner. Do you give the big outfits first chance at the land, or do you sell to anyone at all?"

"You'll get first chance," said the stranger, ducked his head in a little nod, and booted out his beast. Over his shoulder, he called back: "Just don't wait too long is all."

Vern came strolling over where his employer was standing. Together they watched the loner grow small across a white-stained countryside.

"I've met a lot of 'em," muttered Vern. "But never one quite like that before."

Abel said nothing. He had an idea. The more he thought of it, the more sense it made to him. The loner, if what he'd told them was true, definitely favored the big cattle interests. In this day and time, when settlers were pouring westward from an overly populated and economically troubled eastern seaboard, the old-time, long-established cattle barons were under attack from all sides. Their most vulnerable spot was the free-graze land. The government, the army, the clamoring, land-hungry squatters, were all for re-settling these woefully ignorant 'fool-hoe men' upon the cowmen's feudal but unpatented lands.

The loner, whoever he was, whatever had made him as he was, must sometime have been a cowman himself. If, as Abel was thinking as he stood out there in his cold but sun-brightened yard with Vern Patton at his side, if the loner had been one of those cowmen who'd lost their range, and consequently their livelihood, to the squatters, this would account for his attitude now, favoring cattle interests.

Abel turned and started to slowly walk back towards the main house. Perhaps, he told himself, all the care which had been spent upon the loner was not, as his men clearly thought, a total waste of time. Perhaps it was instead a blessing in disguise; one thing Abel knew and had known for over a year now, unless something intervened to save Yellowstone, it was going to go the way of all those other embattled and besieged big ranches whose existences depended entirely upon the free-graze land.

FIVE

Two days later, Abel took John Landon and Vern over to Lincoln with him. It was one of those fine winter days when the sun was reflected upwards off snowdrifts with almost hurting brightness. The air was cold, men's breath steamed and their exposed faces were tight-drawn and pink, but the air smelt good, visibility was perfect, the land lay wonderfully quiet and slumbering. It was one of those winter days, not at all rare, when men left their hearths to be out in it, providing only that they were adequately dressed, which the Yellowstone men were, from bulky riders' coats to gloves.

When they hit town, went slogging through soupy mud to the livery barn, and left their animals there, Lincoln was bustling, noisy, and going about its thriving way, bundled up but cheerful. Three freight wagons, double-tongued and drawn by six big, sweaty horses, came grinding through the underfoot slush from the distant hills, loaded with cordwood.

Abel and his men waited for this ponderous entourage

to pass on by before heading over to the hotel. They were seeking the loner, but at the hotel were informed he was not in. To Abel's query about whether the loner had checked out, the clerk shook his head. He seemed reluctant to discuss the loner.

"He hasn't checked out, Mister Poirer, but he rode off right after breakfast this morning."

"Any idea where he went?"

Again, the clerk shook his head, only this time he didn't utter a word. There was caution in the man's face, caution, doubt, and uncertainty. Abel recognized the signs, and as he was walking back across the lobby, he said to Vern Patton, "I see our friend's affected the folks in Lincoln the same way he affected us at the ranch."

The three of them halted upon the plank walk, were teetering there when a stocky, thin-lipped man also walked out of the hotel lobby. This was Deputy Sheriff Joe Conway, stationed at Lincoln by the Lander County sheriff, who had a policy of placing deputies in the larger towns, thus doing away with the need for the usual town constables while at the same time being sure he was kept informed of everything happening in his bailiwick.

Joe Conway was an ex-cowboy. He was easy-going, affable, and shrewd. It was the shrewdness which brought him out onto the plank walk behind the Yellowstone men. It was also the shrewdness which had led him to sit behind an upraised newspaper in the rearward lobby listening to Abel Poirer's inquiries about the loner.

Joe greeted Vern and John Landon with careless pleasantry, then turned a little less casual when he addressed Abel. "That feller you were askin' about in the hotel," he said to Abel. "The one who's registered as Bill Smith, if you don't mind, Mister Poirer, I'd like to ask you a few questions about him."

Abel gazed at Deputy Conway, said nothing, and nodded. He knew the deputy. He'd never had trouble with him, but upon several occasions, he'd had to bail out troublesome Yellowstone riders—particularly old Puma Partridge—after too much celebrating here in Lincoln.

"Do you know him, Mister Poirer?"

Abel shook his head. "I don't think anyone knows him," he retorted, then recited for Joe Conway everything which had happened since he'd first laid eyes upon the loner.

Conway quietly listened, sucked his teeth, and kept both fisted hands plunged deep into coat pockets. When Abel was finished speaking, the deputy said, "Come with me, Mister Poirer, I'd like to show you something."

He led the Yellowstone men down to a little shed out behind his jailhouse. There was dirty snow banked against the baseboard of this shack, and when Joe Conway unlocked the door and pushed it inward, a rush of bitterly cold air struck the Yellowstone men, along with a peculiar and unpleasant odor of mustiness and strong chemicals.

Conway lit a candle, held it high, walked ahead where something white and thick lay upon a table, raised his candle still higher, drew back the sheet, and disclosed the gray, splotchy, congealed face of a dead man.

"You boys ever see this feller before?" Joe asked.

Vern and John stared. Abel looked down, looked away, looked back for a longer viewing, then wagged his head.

"How about you, Vern? Or you, John?"

Patton also wagged his head. John Landon, seemingly not the least disturbed by this unexpected and grisly sight, said, "Nope. He's a plumb stranger to me, Joe. Who is he?"

Deputy Conway spilt a little wax, set the candle to rest in it, pushed his hands deep into his pockets, hunched his shoulders up against the freezing temperature of this draughty shack, and shook his head.

"Damned if I know. But your friend Bill Smith stopped him cold last night in a saloon."

"Shot him?" asked Abel.

"Yup. Neat as a whistle, too, from what witnesses told me." Conway looked over at Abel. "This one's also named Smith. Now, isn't that a genuine coincidence? Two fellers named Smith arrivin' in Lincoln within a few days of one another, gettin' into a fight the first time they see one another—as near as I can figure it out—and now there's only your Smith left alive."

Vern puckered his face. Beside him, John Landon gazed at the deputy sheriff with quiet curiosity. But it was Abel who spoke next. He said, "I don't understand. What're you driving at, Conway?"

Joe lifted his shoulders, let them fall, and stared at the dead man. "I don't know what I'm driving at. Now that you've seen this one, you fellers know every bit as much as I do about this thing." Joe tugged loose the candle, walked ahead of the others back out of the little shed, blew out the candle, set it upon a fire block, and closed the door. As he re-locked it, he said, "I was hoping you might give me some notion as to what's going on here."

"All I can tell you," responded Abel, "is that the loner said he meant to hang around Lincoln until he found out who shot him." Abel jerked a thumb backward. "Could that man in there be the one?"

Conway straightened up, gazed at the key in his palm, pocketed the thing, and said, "If he did, then he had to be here a month or so back, instead of just riding in the day before he was killed. And also, if he's the one who shot your loner—where's the connection?"

Abel had no answers, so he said, "Your job is to find the answers to those things, Conway."

"Sure, Mister Poirer, and I aim to. But I've got to ask questions in order to get started." Joe looked out over the town with his eyes pinched down against reflected, dazzling sunlight. "And you were my last hope. I've asked around until folks are beginnin' to think all I can ask is questions."

"And—nothing?"

"Not a blessed thing. This here dead man hit town, left his outfit at the livery barn, checked in over at the hotel as Tom Smith, didn't visit anyone that folks recall, and the followin' night in a saloon something passed between this Smith and your Smith—now this one's dead."

Joe looked at the Yellowstone men, his expression wry and wondering. He stamped his booted feet to encourage circulation. He gazed over at Abel Poirer expectantly, as though he thought Yellowstone's owner might have some idea to advance, some suggestion to make.

Abel was, in fact, slowly turning several possible alternate explanations over in his mind, but he had no intention of offering them to Deputy Conway. Not yet, anyway.

"Well," he ultimately said, "you've got yourself a mystery, Deputy," and Abel would have walked off with

Vern and John, but Conway spoke up, delaying this departure.

"This here dead man's belongings are over at my office, Mister Poirer. Would you like to see them?"

Abel seemed to catch an undercurrent in these words of Conway's. He lifted his frosty eyes to Joe's face. "Should I see them?" he softly inquired.

"Yeah, I think so," replied the deputy, and turned to head for the rear entrance into his jailhouse.

Vern and John exchanged a look, hiked along behind their employer, and said not a word until the four of them were inside the stuffy combination office and cell-block, which was Joe Conway's place of business in Lincoln.

Here, Joe stoked up a smoldering fire in his iron stove, tossed in another chunk of pitch-pine, growled something about the cold, and gestured towards some personal effects piled carelessly atop a battered old table.

"That's what was in his saddlebags," Joe said. "Clean socks, pants, two shirts, some extra ammunition…" Joe stepped to his desk, scooped up several crisp white envelopes, and held them up. "And these," he added.

Abel recognized the size and whiteness of those envelopes at once. So did John Landon and Vern Patton. They were identical to the envelopes the loner had also shown them, the envelope containing that homestead patent.

Conway tossed down the envelopes and pushed back his hat. He was staring straight at Abel Poirer. "These here papers, Mister Poirer, are homestead filings on local land."

Abel had a powerful premonition; it kept him from being the least bit surprised at what Conway was saying.

"Can you guess where these claims originated, Mister Poirer?"

"No," said Abel, "but I can guess what land is described in their legal descriptions, Conway."

Joe nodded, shifted his gaze to that little pile of possessions on the table, and softly said, "That's the only thing I've got to go on. The fact that it's Yellowstone range involved in this mess." Without looking up, Joe said, "Mister Poirer, I was goin' to ride out an' see you tomorrow. You see, the way I look at this, there's got to be a lot more to it than a shoot-out between two strangers named Smith. Your range is involved. I reckon a man might even say your livelihood is involved."

Now Conway raised his eyes. They were solemn and skeptical. Vern and John recognized the skepticism. So did Abel Poirer.

"Wait a minute," said Abel. "Conway, if you're thinking I had anything to do with this killing, you're as mistaken as you can be. I told you what the loner said to me the day he left Yellowstone—he was going to hang around until he found the man who'd shot him.

That's the only thing I know at all about this affair."

"Hell, Mister Poirer, I'm not implyin' *you* hired this loner-feller to shoot the other man. All I'm thinkin' is that somewhere, there's a heap more to this than meets the eye, and some way or another it's got to do with Yellowstone land."

Abel said, "I got the impression those two fought a fair fight. Is that right?"

Conway inclined his head. "Every witness I talked to said it was plumb fair. That they both stepped back from the bar an' went for their weapons at the same time, an' the dead feller out in the embalmin' shed just wasn't in the loner's class with six-guns."

"Then," exclaimed Poirer, "you'll hold an inquest, the loner will be exonerated, and that will be that."

"Ordinarily, yes, Mister Poirer, but what's botherin' me isn't just the killin' of this Tom Smith feller, it's what's goin' to happen next. Accordin' to my lights, if those homestead papers get sold around and folks start carvin' up your Yellowstone outfit, there's goin' to be more trouble bust loose in Lander County than a man can shake a stick at. Mister Poirer, I can't quite see you sittin' still for somethin' like that happening. I can't see any big cowman standin' by and seein' everything he's worked a lifetime to build up, go down the drain just like that."

"I'll worry about my own affairs," said Abel coldly.

"All you have to concern yourself with is keeping the peace."

Joe Conway stood there considering Abel. He did not seem in awe of Poirer as so many others were, but he did seem to be considering caution. Joe liked his job, and he'd never been a rash man. He knew perfectly well how powerful Abel Poirer was in Lander County, and even beyond Lander County. He did not fear the Yellowstone outfit, but he certainly would give a lot of serious thought to any action which might seem necessary, but which might antagonize this frosty-eyed, big, and grizzled cowman in front of him.

SIX

Abel was troubled. Back out in the dazzling daylight, he told John and Vern to go buy themselves a drink or two, and as soon as he was alone, Abel crossed through roadway mud to the hotel again. He asked which upstairs room the loner had, got this information, and hiked on up to see whether, during the time he'd been with Joe Conway, the loner had returned.

He hadn't, but his door was not locked, so Abel entered the dingy little room, crossed over to the roadside window, lifted the blind to admit sunlight, took a chair, and sat down to wait. He had no idea how long that wait might be, but neither did he propose to leave town until he'd had a serious talk with the loner.

Putting together in his mind the things which he'd encountered since riding to Lincoln, Abel came up with several obvious observations and several that were not so obvious.

The thing which wasn't so obvious but which loomed largest in his thoughts was the killing of that other mysterious stranger called Tom Smith.

What was obvious was the fact that the loner wasn't the only one engaged in buying homestead claims from potential squatters, then afterwards selling those claims for a profit. This was what kept Abel sitting there as the day ran on; this was what deeply troubled him.

When the loner had explained what he was up to, Abel had found the occupation unique enough to fascinate him; it had never once occurred to him others might also consider this vocation unique—and evidently profitable enough—to also undertake it.

But regardless of who got killed or what strangers came drifting into Lander County, what Joe Conway had said was at the crux of the whole thing as far as Abel Poirer was concerned: He had not spent the best years of his life creating an empire, only to see it go down the drain now because of the homestead laws—or because of these shadowy men who dealt in wholesale homestead land patents. Joe had been correct: Abel would fight for his Yellowstone outfit. If necessary, he would start the fighting right here in this dingy hotel room!

What could these sharp speculators calling themselves 'Smith' know of a dedicated man's feel for the land? How could they fathom what lay deep in the remembering blood of a man whose best years had been dedicated to carving out an empire by sacrifice, by prodigious labor, by sweat and even tears? Could they even begin to comprehend what drove a man such as Abel Poirer had been during those grinding years? Did they suspect how hunger and hardship could drive a boy to lie awake in the bitter nights envisioning his great dream?

Outside, the beautiful sunlight waned, turned reddish out against the far-away mountains, stained snowfields and window-glass the weak color of diluted blood. Abel sat by that overlooking window, his face frozen into a flintiness which had no room for compromise, no hint of anything but bleak austerity. He watched riders come and go, saw ranch rigs, freight wagons, even the afternoon stage come splashing down the muddy roadway, sending pedestrians ducking from gobbets of flying mud.

It was a long vigil. He did not see the man he was watching for turn in over at the livery barn until that enormous red sun was poised inches above a distant saw-edged peak.

He opened his coat, tucked it carefully beneath his shell-belt on the right side, lay a palm lightly upon the startlingly cold butt of his bolstered .45, and waited for the loner to come striding on out of the barn, down through the roadway mud, and up under the window where he waited.

He afterwards swung about to face the door and

listened for heavy footfalls outside. They came, distantly at first, then closer. The door swung inward, the loner bulked large in that opening with his sheepskin coat loose and his hat back on his head. There was the same cold hardness to his face, the same challenging look. He saw Abel sitting over there in thickening shadows and halted stock still.

He returned Abel's unsmiling stare briefly, passed on in, and kicked the door closed behind himself. He said, with sarcasm, "Make yourself at home, Poirer."

With equal irony, Abel said, "Thanks, I will."

The loner shed his coat, cast aside his hat, went over to stir up the coals in his little stove, and while he was busy at this, he said, "You saw Conway. I can see that much in your face, even in this poor light. Now you're beginning to really worry."

"Am I?"

The loner turned to light the lamp. "Yeah," he exclaimed. "And you're also wondering who that dead man was, why we fought, and if there are any more around who might also have homestead papers on Yellowstone range."

"Something like that," murmured Abel, watching the loner.

Lamp glow strengthened against the dingy walls. It lit those two strong faces, making them look evil and harsh.

The loner squared around, draped one hip upon a table, and sat with both hands lying easy in his lap while he watched Poirer's face.

"You've got some kind of an explanation coming, I guess, Poirer. It's your range and your sweat that's been put on the line."

"Thanks," said Abel dryly.

The loner caught that dryness and smiled with his lips, a cold, wolfish smile. He said, "I'll digress a moment, Poirer. In some ways, you and I are alike. Maybe not in the ways folks mostly admire, but at least in ways that make you and me what we are. We're old-fashioned enough to believe in some tarnished ideals."

"Such as?"

"Oh, things like honesty and ethics. Poirer, that dead man Conway probably showed you, he had a different code from you and me. He believed the important thing in life was to make money. He wouldn't actually go outside the law to do it, but he laughed when I mentioned ethics to him. You see, Poirer, he's been copying me for a long time. When I'd get hold of some homestead papers, he'd figure I'd thought the whole thing out, and he'd buy some claims on the same range. His idea was to force contending rangemen to bid against one another for my paper and for his paper. If they didn't want to do that, he'd sell his papers to anyone who'd buy them just to break the big outfits."

"And you," said Abel Poirer. "What exactly were your ethics in this?"

"I thought I'd already made that plain to you. I give the big outfits first crack. I don't hold them up; you pay me my price and you keep your range."

"And if I don't pay it?"

"You will."

Abel stirred in the chair. He pushed out long legs and stared speculatively at his boot toes a moment, then said, "This dead man who called himself Smith—is that what he had in mind, selling my range to someone else?"

"Yes."

"Who?" asked Abel softly, shooting a cold look over at the loner.

"A man named Pat Hennesey. You know Hennesey?"

Abel knew Pat Hennesey, but he didn't admit to it right away. He dropped his gaze to his boot toes again. Hennesey owned the Lincoln Saloon. He was a large, paunchy man with venomous little pig eyes, a man who never overlooked an opportunity to make money. It was not difficult for Abel to comprehend Hennesey's motive in this, either. Pat would buy the homestead claims, resell them at several hundred percent profit to cowboys, squatters, other cowmen, to anyone with the cash to pay for them. Hennesey wouldn't care one bit what this might do to Abel Poirer or the cow empire he'd used the best years of his life to create.

"I know Pat Hennesey," Abel murmured. "Was Smith trying to deal with him?"

"Not exactly. He told me he'd sounded Hennesey out. He also told me I'd better throw in my homestead papers, too. He said if I did that Hennesey would buy the whole she-bang a lot quicker than he'd buy Smith's scattered parcels of land."

"And?"

"I told him you got first call. He laughed at me. I told him what ethics meant." The loner paused, looked out into the settling dusk. "Smith didn't like that. He called me a name."

"And you killed him."

"That's right. But actually, it goes back much farther than this meeting here in Lincoln. He's been doggin' my tracks for two years, doing the same thing. I'd get a deal set up, and he'd come along and throw a wrench into things. Two years is a long time to put up with a man like Smith."

"Was that his name?"

"No, but that's not important."

Abel cocked his head at the loner. He thought he knew the kind of answer he'd get to his next question, but he tried anyway. "Loner, what's behind your ethics? I mean, why do you favor the cow outfits over the squatters?"

The loner got up, went to his sheepskin, dug out a cigar, lit it over the lamp chimney, puffed up a good head of smoke, and went on back to ease down upon the table again.

"You know the answer you ought to get to that question, don't you?" he said.

"Yeah, I know, and I'm expecting it."

The loner removed his cigar, studied its glow, and trimmed some uneven ash with his little finger. "Once I had an outfit, Poirer," he softly said. "That was a few years back. I also had a wife. As pretty a woman as a man ever laid eyes on. Kind, too, like your Nettie is."

The loner replaced his cigar between strong teeth and bit hard down on it. He did not look at Abel, but beyond him out into the faintly lit evening.

"We put in seven years building things up. In another seven, we'd have had what you've got at Yellowstone. It takes a lot of work, a lot of sweat and sacrifice, and like you, I was so busy makin' it work, makin' it grow, I never saw the handwriting on the wall. We heard of that homestead law, but hell, we were too busy to take time out to stop a moment and see what it might do to us.

"Well, they came. Not just a few wagons of 'em, but by the dozens. Mostly they couldn't speak English, couldn't even sit a saddle, or clean a water-hole. But they had their land patents; a hundred and sixty acres smack-dab in the middle of my range. They fenced off my water, my winter feed. They ploughed up the springtime grass.

"Poirer, you know how long it took them to ruin me; how long did it take them to ruin you? *One year!* That's how long, one damned year, and you see everything you've had and everything you've dreamed of having, just wiped out."

Abel stirred again in the chair. The stove had gone out. Nighttime chill was seeping through the walls. The loner's face showed suffering and anguish. His naked soul was bared, and this embarrassed Abel, so he kept leaning downward, staring at the floor.

"Their first winter was a bad one, Poirer. Drifts four feet high. Those people found out too late that you can't make a living on a lousy hundred and sixty acres of rangeland. They starved, so they took to killin' a beef now and then. I caught three and I hanged 'em, but that wasn't the answer. Anyway, come spring, I was finished—wiped out. Also, come spring, my wife died of lung-fever, what they call tuberculosis nowadays."

Abel got stiffly upright, went over and worried the stove, coaxed up a little flame, and chucked more wood into the fire-box. He then returned to his chair, but he didn't sit down. He instead turned his back on the loner and stood gazing solemnly down into the lamp-lighted roadway. There was a stifling moment of bitter quiet, then someone rapped sharply upon the corridor door, and a voice Abel instantly recognized called through.

"Mister Poirer, you in there? You all right?"

Abel turned from the waist. "I'm here, Vern. Listen, you and John go on home. Tell Mrs. Poirer I'm staying in town tonight."

Vern's low mumble came for a moment as he and Landon discussed something, then Vern called out again. "You sure you're all right in there?"

Abel and the loner exchanged a look. The cowman apologetically smiled, crossed over, and opened the door. "I'm fine," he said. "Do like I said, Vern."

Vern and John Landon craned around to see the loner perched back there in the little room with a dead cigar between his lips. Vern muttered, "All right, Mr. Poirer. Anything else?"

"No. I'll come home tomorrow."

Abel closed the door, stood with his back to it, gazing across at the loner, then said, "All right, I kind of had an idea it was something like this. You had to have some notion about loyalty to cattle interests to talk as you did, Loner, unless you were talkin' through your hat, and that's why I waited in here for you today. To determine which it was, with you."

"And now you know, Poirer."

"Yes. And now I'm wondering why you didn't tell Joe Conway at least that part of it about you and Smith being old enemies."

"First off, it's none of Conway's business. Secondly, I found out something interesting during my talk with Smith. He was here in Lincoln the day after I arrived here a month back."

"Joe Conway doesn't know that. In fact, he's sure Smith's never been in his bailiwick before."

"Well, he's wrong. Smith let that slip while we were arguing in Hennesey's saloon."

"I see. And you think Smith may be the man who shot you."

The loner shrugged. "Hell busted loose before I could dig that far. He could've done it, Poirer, but he'd never have done it on his own. You see, in a way, I was the goose that laid the golden eggs for Smith. I did all the groundwork of gettin' the original land patents. That's how it's always been between us. I'd get the papers for a particular stretch of range, then Smith'd move in right behind me and buy adjoining pieces of land. No, Smith wouldn't have tried to kill me just for the hell of it."

"And now you want to know why he tried it—if in fact it was Smith who did try it."

"Wouldn't you?"

"I suppose I would," murmured Abel. "There's one other question I want answered, Loner: How much are you going to hold me up for the other land patents you have to my range?"

"I have fifteen of 'em, Poirer, and I want a thousand dollars each for 'em."

Abel stood there gazing at the younger man. Fifteen thousand dollars was a lot of money. He had it—he had many times that much—but it stuck in his craw that the loner had bought those patents for a pittance.

"You said you gave from ten to a hundred dollars apiece for those parcels, Loner."

"Yeah," assented the younger man. "Sometimes I even hire cowboys to go in and file, then bring me the papers, and I pay them for their time. It takes 'em maybe an hour to fill out the filing notices, get their patents, and bring 'em to me. At a hundred dollars an hour, they make damned good pay. At that rate, Poirer, you're gettin' off dirt cheap."

The loner removed his cigar, saw that it was chewed ragged, walked over, and threw it into the merrily popping little stove. He turned with his back to that welcome warmth and spoke.

"A man usually pays more for his oversights than he pays for his experiences, Poirer. You could've saved your range if you hadn't been so content to sit out there at Yellowstone bein' a rich land baron." The loner shrugged. "Besides, you've got enough money to retire on by now. Let the damned squatters have the range, sell your cattle, and take it easy in your sun-down years. You've got no heirs to fight for anyway."

"Haven't I?" said Abel. "Who told you that?"

"No one. I was at your place for a month, and all I ever saw out there was you, Mrs. Poirer, and your riders."

"I've got a daughter, Loner. She's got a little boy."

"Well, I didn't know about that."

"It's none of your business."

"No," agreed the loner. "All right, pay the fifteen thousand and keep Yellowstone intact for your daughter and her husband—and your grandson."

"I'll think about it."

The loner's face turned sardonic. "Don't take too long," he murmured, "or your son-in-law'll have no inheritance to keep intact for your daughter, Poirer."

"My son-in-law," said Abel Poirer, "is dead. My daughter is a widow. I'll let you know what I decide in the morning. Good night."

SEVEN

The loner was standing outside a café the following morning with his sheepskin unbuttoned, his hat back on his head, and his six-gun plainly visible and handy, when Joe Conway emerged from the stage office, saw him, and walked on over.

Joe had no illusions about the loner. In his own way, Conway was every bit as good a judge of men as Abel Poirer was. Joe nodded, got back a long, steady look, and said, "Couple of questions. First off, who's goin' to pay for Tom Smith's burial, an' is that the name we ought to put on his headstone? The other question is— what was Smith up to, with all those homestead claims in his possession? Because you see, accordin' to the law, a man can't prove-up on but one homestead at a time."

"If that's the law," replied the loner, "then don't worry about Smith tryin' to break it—even if he was alive to do it."

"I'm not worrying," said Conway. "Curious would be more like it."

The loner looked southward along the slushy roadway. It had been bitterly cold the night before; there were sharp-edged little daggers of ice here and there in the crunchy mud, and thus far in the day, that overhead dazzling sun hadn't generated enough heat to melt them. Conway followed out the loner's line of vision, saw nothing important, and got the idea that the husky man beside him was not going to answer him.

"Well," Joe said, after a while, "I guess a man can only do just so much in his attempts to be friendly, feller, then he has to change his tactics."

This quiet-spoken, unmistakable threat brought the loner's wintry gaze around. He stood waiting for Conway to elaborate on this, and Joe obliged him.

"We've got a town ordinance in Lincoln that says when there's been a gunfight, the survivor's got to leave town and stay away for six months. It's not a bad ordinance, Mister Smith. It's designed to keep feuds from perpetuatin' themselves in Lincoln and maybe gettin' the townspeople shot up."

"No one's going to avenge Tom Smith, Deputy."

"Maybe not, but that ordinance has teeth for other reasons too."

"Like gettin' rid of undesirables, Deputy?"

Joe Conway smiled without mirth. "Right on the nose with that guess," he drawled.

The loner stood there studying Conway for a long

time. Without another word, he stepped down into the mud and went slogging on across the road towards the livery barn.

Conway watched him go. He scratched the tip of his rather long nose, said a mild swear word under his breath, and turned as Abel Poirer came up and halted, also looking over where the loner was hiking along.

"Leave him alone," Abel said. "He's broken no laws, Deputy."

"Sorry, Mister Poirer. I just suggested that he ride on out and stay away."

Abel swung and looked down his nose. "By what authority did you do that? He killed Smith in a fair fight."

Conway explained about the ordinance. He concluded by saying that he didn't propose to have any unsolved mysteries in his town, and if the loner didn't want to explain what he was doing in Lincoln and why he'd killed Tom Smith, then Joe Conway didn't want him around.

To all this, Abel Poirer had a tart reply. "You're not running him out of town, Deputy. If you want to buck me too, just try it."

Joe looked quizzically at the iron-like older man. He said mildly, "Mister Poirer, I sure don't want to fight you."

"Then don't push for it, Deputy."

"But I sure will fight you. You, an' Yellowstone, and this mysterious killer Bill Smith, too, if I have to."

"You don't have to, Conway. Just stay out of the way for a few days."

"What good'll that do?"

"It'll save a lot of trouble, not only for you but for all of us."

"Mind explainin' that, Mister Poirer?"

"Yes, I mind explaining it. I can't explain it. If I do—if word gets out what's going on here—you'll have more trouble explode in Lander County than you ever thought possible. And one more thing: I'm going over to the county seat today to see the sheriff. I'm going to ask him to instruct you to impound those homestead claims you took off that dead man. I'm also going to ask him to tell you not to say a word about those papers to anyone at all."

Joe Conway fished a limp tobacco sack from his inside shirt pocket. He carefully extracted a rice paper, troughed it, measured out the correct amount of tobacco, and went to work fashioning a smoke. By the time he had the thing lit, he'd come to a decision in his mind and said mildly, "Mister Poirer, I'll save you a long, cold ride. You tell me the answer to just one thing, and I'll lock those papers in my office safe and keep their existence a secret from my own wife."

"What is it you want to know?"

"Is Pat Hennesey involved in this?"

"He is."

Joe Conway smoked and looked out over his town. "Now we're gettin' somewhere," he muttered under his breath. "Now I'm beginnin' to sink my teeth into something."

Abel, in the act of stepping down off the plank walk into that cold and sluggish roadway mud, paused to look over at the lithe lawman.

"Explain that," he said crisply.

Conway heeded the sharpness of that order but not right away, not until he'd removed his smoke and flicked ash off it. Then he said, speaking slowly and quietly, "Pat was at my place last night. He never said what he wanted exactly, only that the dead man had some papers belongin' to him."

Abel's expression turned suddenly hard. Conway, seeing this, gently bobbed his head up and down.

"Those homestead papers o' course, Mister Poirer. I figured that's what it was, but until you just now told me Pat was involved, I had my doubts."

"What did you tell him, Deputy?"

"Nothing. What could I tell him? He never came right out and said what the papers were." Conway made a slow, sly smile. "Mister Poirer, you live seventeen miles west of Lincoln, but even so, you know Pat Hennesey. Well, sir, I see him just about every blessed day, so I also know him.

Maybe even a little better than you do, an' knowin' him as I do makes it possible for me to sometimes second-guess him. Unless I'm sure wrong, Pat was dealin' for those papers with the dead man. He had in mind blackmailin' you into buyin' them, or maybe he had in mind ruining your range by selling them to those settlers who come drivin' through every now and then. He could maybe even sell them to other cowmen hereabouts, although I sure doubt that. But one thing I'm sure of—he'd use them any way he could to hurt you."

"You're pretty handy at guessing," said Abel, with his cold gaze fixed upon Conway. "Now do you understand why you've got to keep quiet about this? If you don't, if the word spreads that anyone can buy a piece of Yellowstone range for a few dollars, squatters will charge in here like maniacs to buy those claims."

"I understand, Mister Poirer. That's why I just said I'd lock the things up and keep my mouth closed about 'em."

Abel and Joe Conway stood gazing at one another for a long time. Finally, the cold, aloof, rich cowman slowly removed a glove and pushed out his right hand.

"I never forget a favor," he murmured, and after he and Deputy Conway had shaken hands, Abel turned and went across to the livery barn where the loner was just emerging astride a rented horse but riding his own scarred Saddle.

"Where are you going?" Poirer bluntly asked.

The loner said, "For a ride. What difference does it make?"

"It might make a lot of difference," exclaimed Abel. He swung, bawled at a shuffling hostler down in the barn, and snapped for that man to fetch him a saddled horse at once. As the hostler looked up, saw who had given this order, and sprang to obey it, Abel squared back around towards the loner.

"We've got some dickering to do, Loner. Fifteen thousand is too high."

"Is it?" asked the mounted man, his face blank but his voice faintly interested, faintly amused. "How does a man arrive at a cash price for survival?"

"By figuring what it's going to cost him."

"And I say it'll cost you fifteen thousand."

Abel shook his head. "Way too much," he reiterated. "But we'll discuss it as we ride along."

"How do you know we're going the same direction, Poirer?"

"We are," stated Abel, and turned to accept the reins as that hostler came prancing up leading a rigged-out livery animal. Abel dropped a coin into the hostler's lingering hand, mounted, and looked across. The loner returned that look and shrugged.

"All right. As it happens, I was heading for the Devil's Postpile, so you were right; we *are* riding in the same direction."

They passed northward up out of Lincoln side by side, saying nothing, and hunching up against the wintertime bite. Joe Conway stood over where he'd been before, watching those two depart from Lincoln. Joe still had his dead cigarette between his lips. His gaze was speculative, but it was also knowing. He didn't know as much as he'd like to know about all this, but he certainly knew a lot more than he had the day before, and to a man of Joe's consistent temperament that was an auspicious opener.

What he'd deliberately neglected to tell the man who called himself Bill Smith was that his primary concern about Pat Hennesey's involvement in this matter of free-graze land centered around Pat's having suddenly imported two men to work for him over at the Lincoln Saloon—men who wore tied-down hand-guns, and who, although they functioned now as bartenders, were about as unlikely a pair of drink dispensers as Joe had ever seen.

Crafty Pat Hennesey was up to something; it wasn't anything respectable, Joe would bet a new Stetson on that, and Pat was entirely too fond of money to pay the wages of two hired gunfighters just because he needed additional bartenders. Pat was up to something, and that 'something' involved those homestead papers in Joe's office, so Joe finally turned to saunter on over to his office to lock up those papers as he'd promised Poirer he'd do. He also meant to go have a long talk with Pat Hennesey, too, but there wasn't any big hurry about that. Pat had been Joe's private headache for a long time. As he walked along now, he wondered if this time, Pat would come up the loser. He sincerely hoped so.

EIGHT

Abel and the loner wrangled over the price Poirer had to pay for the land patents nearly all the way out to that part of Yellowstone range where nature had planted a boulder field with some stalactite-type fluted columns that leaned into one another, and which were the cause for this area being known among the cowmen as the Devil's Postpile.

The weather held, but off in the north, there were dirty clouds building up one above the other, huge and ragged and threatening. Where the sun struck hard against them, these clouds showed a sifting of ominous gray which hardened into a gunpowder color.

"Storm's buildin' up," observed the loner, but Abel was not interested.

"Listen to me," he said, as they swung in closer to the boulder field. "Five thousand is much more than you gave. It's a good profit, Loner."

"Fifteen's better, Poirer."

"Last night you said you didn't hold folks up."

"I don't. Fifteen thousand is dirt cheap." The loner waved a heavily sleeved arm. "Where else could a man come by so much good grassland for fifteen thousand?"

The loner dropped his arm, reined over into the boulder field, and halted. He sat there looking down, his expression altering, becoming absorbed with whatever was in his mind.

"Right here is where I got shot."

Abel looked, recognized the spot, and ran his gaze around. At his side, the loner dismounted, walked ahead a few feet, and halted again, this time loosely holding his horse's reins and with his back to Abel.

"Come here, Poirer," he ordered.

Abel rode on up without dismounting, folded his gauntleted hands atop the saddle horn, and sat there looking disgruntled. The loner turned to gaze up at him.

"I came out here yesterday," he said. "It's always stuck in my craw—why would a man be hidin' in here an' shoot a perfect stranger for also comin' here?"

Abel sat on, looking and saying nothing.

"I'll tell you why, Poirer," went on the Loner. "Because there was something here, and because that bushwhacker was out here either to guard it, or to get it."

Abel grunted. "What makes you think anyone was here ahead of you? The way my riders and I have it figured, you were already here when someone came up and shot you."

"Yeah, I know," replied the loner. "I knew that's how you boys figured it from listenin' to you at the bunkhouse. But you see, I knew a damned sight better."

"Then why didn't you tell us?"

"Naw. I wanted to see if any of you'd make a slip and admit bein' out here ahead of me. I didn't know who shot me, and I wanted to know." The loner faced fully around, planted his feet apart, and hooked his rein-hand in his belt as he gazed upwards. "You see, Poirer, *I was here*—you fellers weren't here. So I know how I got shot. You fellers don't know."

The loner waited a while for Abel to comment, but Abel never did, so the loner turned and pointed at something at the base of an immense boulder. "Get down, Poirer," he said. "Step up and take a look here."

Abel obeyed, curious now and interested. He walked slightly ahead of the loner, bent and ran a careful stare along the eroded base of that granite monolith. There was an unmistakable hole in one place. Even the snowfall which had intervened between the time of the loner's shooting and now had not been able to obscure marks of earnest digging here.

Abel went up even closer, dropped to one knee, and put forth a hand to test that moist earth. It crumbled, showing little raw-edged flakes of granite which had been chipped from the big boulder by something wielded by strong arms.

Behind him, the loner said, "Satisfied, Poirer?"

Abel twisted to look back. The loner was near smiling, his eyes were like wet agate, and his lips were drawn back a little from square, even white teeth.

"There was something buried here," exclaimed Abel. He got back upright and frowned. "I'm beginning to understand," he murmured.

The loner unbuttoned his coat, dug around inside for a cigar, lit up, and exhaled a bluish cloud. He still looked pleased about something.

"Loner, I think you're right. I think there *was* someone here. You rode up, interrupted him—whoever he was— and he shot you."

"That's ancient history," said the loner. "What intrigues me is this: What was buried here?"

Abel shook his head. This suddenly revealed secret had taken him entirely by surprise; he could not yet begin to speculate.

"And," went on the loner. "Who hid it, who dug it up, and where is it now, whatever it is?"

Abel turned to ask softly: "Have you another of those cigars?"

The loner looked mildly surprised. "Yes," he answered. "But I didn't know you smoked. Never saw you smoke."

"I don't ordinarily," said Abel, and accepted the cigar,

leaned into the light the loner offered, and settled back again, still scowling perplexedly at that hole under the boulder.

"You got any ideas?" the loner asked.

"No, none at all. This upsets all my other notions about your shooting."

"Well," said the loner quietly, "I was a little puzzled too, until yesterday. Since then, I've been doin' some thinking. Tell me something, how well do you know that garrulous old cuss at Yellowstone named Puma Partridge?"

Abel's head whipped around. "No," he said instantly and violently. "You're wrong; I'll stake a fortune on it. Puma's been around too many years for me not to know him like the inside of a book. He wouldn't be involved in anything like this. Troublesome he may be at times, windy and truculent even—but not dishonest."

The loner nodded, puffed a moment, then said, "I was afraid of that. It'd be a lot simpler if he had a hand in this someway. I could sweat it out of him."

"That was a coincidence, him riding over here the day you were shot. But he's been ridin' out looking at the cattle for years, summer and winter, and since critters often come over here to get in among these boulders when they smell a storm coming, it was natural for him to check this place." Abel paused, looked at the hole briefly, then looked back up at the loner. "As a matter of fact, if it hadn't been for Puma, you'd be dead right now."

"All right," conceded the loner. "All right, no need to get upset. I'm just floundering around looking for something. He was an idea, that's all."

"You'll have to look elsewhere. "

"I already have, Poirer. I looked all over this country yesterday. Know what I came up with? An idea on how to smoke someone out into the open."

"Who?"

The loner shrugged. "I don't know who. Not yet. But listen for a minute, then tell me what's wrong with this notion of mine. Someone had something hidden here. He wasn't in any hurry to dig it up an' remove it. Maybe he figured to leave it hidden here until spring, or maybe even next summer. If that wasn't so—if something didn't scare him bad about this spot—why did he come out here to dig it up that particular day, with a bad storm brewing and when it was dangerous to be ridin' out?"

Abel said nothing. The loner hadn't expected him to, evidently, because he now answered his own question.

"I'll tell you. Because that feller heard what I was in Lincoln to do—sell this same parcel of land. Remember, Poirer, I rode in the day before I was shot. Remember something else, too: Tom Smith rode in the day after— and right away, he got to talkin' around at the Lincoln

Saloon. Now, then—the very next day, when I rode out to see what this land of mine looked like, some other man was already out here digging up his secret, and he was plenty worried. He was diggin' so frantically, he didn't hear me until I was almost onto him. That's when he fired. He didn't look at me close, he just cut loose. And another thing, Poirer: it was windy as the devil that day, visibility was mighty poor, and it was cold enough to chill the marrow in a man's gun hand. Those things combined, plus that feller's almighty big hurry, were what kept him from killing me outright."

When the loner finished speaking, he had to strike a fresh match and relight his cigar. He looked out at Abel over cupped hands as he did this. He seemed to be awaiting reaction and comment. He got both.

Abel pushed out a name. "Hennesey!" His expression turned fierce. "What you've said just now leads to only one man: Pat Hennesey."

The loner let smoke dribble past his lips while he watched Abel's expression turn bleak. He, too, had come to this identical conclusion, but it had clearly been his wish to have this substantiated by someone else.

"All right," he now said in quiet agreement. "We've got part of it figured out. Suppose we do a little more figuring."

But Abel shook his head. He was a direct man, and

theorizing had no appeal for him. He crossed over to his horse, toed in, and sprang up. "It's too cold to stand around here talking," he said, "and just talking isn't going to produce anything." Abel cast a look at that bitter northerly sky. He pursed his lips tentatively, then said, "Come along, we'll head for Yellowstone. We'd never make it back to Lincoln now anyway. Seventeen miles is too far. That storm'll catch us."

The loner smoked and considered the changing sky. He made no comment, but ultimately went to his animal, mounted, and reined out after Abel. He had nothing to say for almost half an hour. By then, the Yellowstone buildings were in sight beneath that swift-running, darkening, wild-night sky. It was not yet late afternoon, but day was dimming all around, the world was taking on an ominous, steely hue, and the cold was steadily building up towards a bitter freeze.

"Poirer," said the loner. "What would a man have hidden under that big stone?"

"I have no idea."

"Well, have there been any robberies hereabouts, any holdups?"

"Not that I've heard of. But then I probably wouldn't hear anyway. We'll return to town tomorrow. Joe Conway'll have those answers."

The loner had to content himself with this because Abel did not say anything further.

They came down into the windy Yellowstone yard with their faces in behind turned-up coat-collars. That raw, biting wind turned the skin red and tender, flying dust particles cut like tiny knives as they got down, led their animals into the barn, and paused there to slowly relax bunched-up, sluggish bodies.

Out of a gloomy place, a lank cowboy hiked forward, peered at those two, then dolefully wagged his head at them. This was Puma Partridge; he had been 'choring'—feeding the stalled animals and doing the other multiple odd-jobs which required doing around a cow-outfit barn lot morning and night. Puma had his bearskin coat on, turned up, and he also had someone's ancient, soiled shawl wrapped over the top of his big-brimmed hat, down over his ears, and loop-thru-knotted under his jaw. He was, any time, a figure to inspire humor, but attired as he now was, and squinting up close at Abel Poirer and the loner, old Puma looked like some disreputable old banshee.

The loner's normally cold gaze fell upon him and lingered for as long as it took the loner to turn down his collar, ease back his hat, and blow out a big breath of steamy air. Then the loner grinned.

No one at Yellowstone had ever before seen the loner genuinely smile. Puma looked, approved, made a raffish grin of his own, and said in his chirping, garrulous way: "Loner, I declare you look right close to bein' human when you smile." Then old Puma reared back, looked at his employer, shuffled his feet, and said: "Mister Poirer, good thing you got back, otherwise Miz' Nettie'd have sent someone into town after you."

Abel, in the act of off-saddling, grew suddenly still and apprehensive. "What is it?" he called forth, making sure Puma could hear him over the oncoming storm.

"Miss Toni's here."

Abel straightened fully around. The loner looked, saw amazement on Abel's face, and swung to see what Puma would do now.

The old cowboy's features screwed up mightily. He popped his head up and down like a cork in a tub of water. "Sure, Mister Poirer. She come in last night on the late stage, her'n the little boy. She hired a town rig to fetch her on out here. Arrived around two, three o'clock this mornin.'"

Abel tossed the tag-end of his latigo at Puma. "Finish up here," he ordered, turned, and without a word or a glance at the loner, went hastening on out of the barn.

The loner strolled up just far enough to see Abel bending into the increasingly wild, dark day's fury, on his way over to the main house. He didn't hear Puma call to him protestingly about being left to care for both their animals, not until Puma bellowed like a bull, then the loner turned back to care for his animal.

Puma finished with Abel's horse, cocked his head,

and said, "You fellers just made it. She's goin' to be a wild one tonight for sure."

The loner ignored this. "Who is Miss Toni?" he asked.

Puma blinked. "Miss Toni? Why hell, man, she's Mister Poirer's daughter. I figured everyone would know that."

"Well, now, how the hell would I know it?" growled the loner and darkly scowled over at Puma. "Go on over to the bunkhouse and stoke up the fire. I'll be along in a minute."

NINE

There was something in the wild sky that held the loner stationary in the barn's big doorless opening for a while, something violent and powerful and troubled. It was as though the world around him was reflecting an identical bitterness, an identical rebellion, to the same kind of emotion which lived within him, too; had lived within him since the death of his wife and the dissolution of his big dream.

He was still there when the world grew dark with an acrid smell to it, wind hammered at roof-shingles and caused that mighty log barn to groan and creak upon its foundation-logs.

He had no idea how much time had elapsed. When daylight winked out long before evening, and swirling gloom came racing down from the howling north borne along upon the convolutions of a terrible wind. He only knew, after a while, that all this dark wildness had woven through its wildest strainings an infinite sadness.

He felt this, was attuned to it, so he did not at once realize that someone was out in the punishing night with him until bobbing lamplight snagged his attention to where someone was battling their way towards the barn from Abel Poirer's residence.

Expecting Abel, the loner was surprised when Nettie Poirer appeared, moved past into the barn out of the buffeting wind, lowered the hood of her cloak, and held up the lantern so that its steady yellow brightness touched the loner's face.

He admired Nettie Poirer. She was smaller than his wife had been and a good fifteen, maybe twenty, years older, but there was something fathomless which reminded him of that other woman.

"You shouldn't be standing out here, Mister Smith," the small, dark-eyed woman said. "The men have supper ready at the bunkhouse. Why don't you join them?"

He nodded at her, wondering what she, also, was doing out of the house. "Directly," he said. "I'm not so hungry I can't take a moment out to see an' hear the dark beauty of all this violence."

She stood still watching his face for a moment longer, then lowered the lantern, looked out and around, drew her cape closer, and nodded. "I know," she murmured so softly he scarcely caught it. "I do this often."

"Do what, ma'am?"

She tilted her head a little, keening this wild night. "Go out into storms, Mister Smith. You lose something by remaining indoors on nights like this. You lose sight of nature's power, her unleashed ferocity. I think if every great man had to stand out in a storm once or twice a year, he'd understand perhaps just how frail men are and how humble they ought to be but seldom are."

The loner put one shoulder against the doorway as he gazed down at that small, handsome woman. An emotion stirred deep in him which he could not define, but it was close to comprehension. He kept watching her, wondering about her. Thinking he knew what she meant.

He said, "Life has a way of humbling folks, Mrs. Poirer. If you were thinkin' of your husband just now when you said men ought to be humble and seldom are, let me tell you—he's being humbled right now. Not by this storm, but by another kind of storm—the kind that doesn't make a sound."

She swung to face the loner. "He told us, Mister Smith, about the possibility of losing all our free-graze land. That's the storm you mean, isn't it?"

"Yes'm."

"And you're part of that storm."

The loner nodded, saying nothing. Uneasiness filled him as Nettie Poirer's liquid dark eyes lingered. It occurred to him that if Abel had told this woman and her daughter about some things, he'd very likely told them about other things as well; about the loner, for instance, and he didn't like this because, by nature, he shrank from pity of any kind.

He straightened up off the barn, reached up to tug low his hat, and would have gone away, but Nettie Poirer spoke again.

"Mister Smith, I came out here looking for you."

He knew what was coming. This woman had twice tried to mother him when he'd been bedfast in the bunkhouse. He reacted now as he'd reacted then.

"Never mind me," he said quickly. "I'm near thirty years old. For all those years, I've been looking out for myself. I don't need your sympathy, Miz' Poirer, and I don't want it."

"Wait, just let me say one thing, Mister Smith. I, too, have lived a number of years, and life is a good teacher. Mister Smith, when a man loses everything, it's very easy for him to also lose his own identity, to become bitter and indifferent and callous. But that doesn't happen to wise men or good men; it only happens with narrow-minded, self-centered men. You aren't either of those things—or are you, Mister *Smith?*"

He caught her emphasis on his nameless name; he also understood that Abel had told her all about him. He stood a moment gazing down into her face, his bitterness like gall, and for this brief moment, he was angry towards her husband.

He touched his hat brim in a little salute to her and said softly over the gusty run of the wind, "Miz' Poirer, there are lots of women in this world, but I think, of a very special kind of women, there have been very, very few—maybe just my wife… and you. Good night."

He left her standing small and cape-shrouded in the barn opening, her hand-lantern casting an immense shadow backwards. He fought his way to the bunkhouse, shouldered open the door, and quickly stepped inside. Puma Partridge let out a squawk and shielded the wildly fluttering lamp with his shapeless old hat.

"Close the danged door," he croaked at the loner. "Set the bar on it."

The others were eating. They turned to cast speculative looks upwards, but they said nothing, and only their casually careful nods indicated that they even recognized their guest.

Puma went to the stove, heaped a dish with some stew he'd concocted which defied analysis, returned with this plate to the table, and put the stew at an empty place. "Take off your hat," he said to the loner. "Shed your coat an' eat up, boy. I got a feelin' you're goin' to be with us a spell." Puma dropped his head, shoveled in food, then sat straight up as a fresh thought struck him. "Hey, after supper, we could maybe work us up a little game of stud-poker. What say, fellers?"

John Landon shot Puma a look, resumed eating, and said nothing. Drew Ruddabaugh, the youngest and least reserved, wrinkled his nose at Puma. "Sure," he assented, "if you'll agree to sit directly under the light this time."

Vern Patton looked swiftly at Drew, then on over at Puma. Everyone's attention left the loner at once; Drew's remark and its implication of cheating had not been missed. Puma straightened up over there, turned and put a sharp gaze at Ruddabaugh, but before he could collect his thoughts sufficiently to speak, dark Martin Caine said, "I got a better idea: let's *both* you fellers sit under that cussed light."

The loner, easing down at the table, saw the fire go out of old Puma and put in his own two-bits worth to also dilute the resentment here.

"All I've got is gold coins," he said. "But if you boys have no objection to that, I'd like a good game of poker."

Cupidity was a strong instinct among inveterate poker players like the Yellowstone men—like all professional cowboys, in fact. Men who never saw gold and didn't actually ever see very much silver money could forget all about a near-insult as they turned now to covertly speculate upon the gambling prowess, or lack of it, eating supper with them in that odorous old log bunkhouse with the storm outside making the building shiver and groan. Martin Caine got up, fetched back the big coffee pot, and went along to the loner's place to solicitously inquire if the guest wished more java. Vern Patton offered his tobacco sack, and the loner hid a raffish smile. Sometimes a good move had fringe benefits; all he'd meant to do was take the sting out of thoughtless words, but it seemed that he'd also made these simple, forthright men completely forget their own earlier coolness towards him.

He accepted the coffee with a grateful nod. He even accepted Vern's sack of makings, although he rarely ever smoked cigarettes, and he privately thought that if he had to forfeit ten or twenty dollars to these men, it was a small price to pay.

But this jarred him. It had been a very long time since the loner had felt benign towards others. A longer time since he'd evaluated the feelings of others and had bent his own feelings to be in tune. He worked up the smoke, lit it, dropped his face, and heard an inner something. A recollection of Nettie Poirer's words came to him as bell-clear and verbatim as though she were there to repeat them.

"Hey," crowed old Puma, jumping up from the table. "Listen to that cussed storm. I'll chuck another piece of fir in the stove and fetch the cards. You fellers clear off the table."

Puma was halfway to the stove when something

heavy struck the door, clawed and punched at it, then a man's voice rose up muffled and wind-whipped.

"Lift the bar!"

Vern, being closest and recognizing Abel's voice, jumped to obey. Again, that overhead hanging lamp swayed wildly as a lunging chunk of the wild night got past, and again Puma jumped to shield the guttering flame until the door was fought closed again.

Abel had shaved and was freshly dressed, but his rangeman's sheepskin coat was the same. He stood there a moment catching his breath, looking around at all those upturned, waiting faces, then he said, "Loner, I'd like to talk to you. Come on over to the main house with me."

Puma's long face grew longer. "Mister Poirer," he protested, "we was just fixin' to have a little friendly set-to."

Abel said nothing as the loner stood up, reached for his hat, his coat, and half twisted to look at old Puma as he shrugged into these garments. He fished inside his coat as he'd done once before, brought out a coin which glinted with an evil light, flipped it over, and made a little tough smile.

"Play for me," he said. "And Puma—remember, that's fifty dollars. I get half of your winnings."

Abel opened the door, eased through, followed by the loner, held the latch until someone inside threw solid weight against the panel, and dropped the bar. Then Abel let go, set himself to buck the night back across the yard, and would have shouldered past except that the loner caught his arm, detaining him there upon the stingy little bunkhouse porch with its creaking overhang.

"Say what you've got to say right here, Poirer," growled the loner. "I'm not goin' over there to be exhibited to your wife and daughter for their pity and curiosity."

Poirer's eyes, about all that was visible from behind his turned-up collar, showed surprise. He seemed momentarily at a loss, so the loner spoke again.

"You told them about me, what I told you in my room at the hotel. Thanks a lot for that, Poirer. I reckon I'm not such a good judge of men after all. I had you pegged for a feller who knew when to talk an' when not to."

Poirer reached up with one gauntleted hand, brushed aside his turned-up collar, and said, "I had a reason for saying what I did. I think it was a good reason."

"Yeah," mumbled the loner. "Gets pretty tame around ranch houses in the wintry nights. I know how that is. Any gossip is better'n just sittin' around lookin' at one another."

"Listen, Loner, my daughter just arrived."

"I heard about that the same time you did."

Poirer acted as though he hadn't been interrupted.

"She's been living in Denver for the past three years. That's where her husband died of lung fever."

"What's that got to do with—?"

"Shut up and listen," snapped Abel Poirer. "When I was telling my wife and daughter about that place at Devil's Postpile where someone had buried something, my daughter told *me* something. Within the past six months, there have been four bullion robberies on the Denver-Cheyenne stage run. Altogether, thirty thousand dollars has been stolen."

"But Denver's a long way from—"

"I said shut up and listen. Posses have scoured the country down there and found nothing—except tracks leading north made by two men. Every time they've lost the tracks, and the men, down at Cotati." Abel paused to gaze at the loner. "You make anything out of that?" he eventually asked.

"I'm beginning to," said the loner. "Cotati's about sixty miles south of Lincoln. I know, because I passed through there on my way up here."

"Then," pronounced Abel, "Denver *isn't* so far from here after all, is it?"

Those two stood staring at one another for a long moment while the wind beat around them, cold came to tighten the flesh of their faces and bring water to their eyes.

Finally, the loner said, "Hennesey again?"

Abel shook his head. "Who knows? Maybe it's not even a close guess, but for lack of anything better, it won't hurt to think about it. Now come on over and talk to my daughter. She knows most of the details of those robberies. She says that's all the folks down in Denver have been talking about for the past half a year."

Abel turned, stepped down onto the freezing ground, and started leaning forward into the punishing wind. Behind him, the loner also moved out, but he went along at a slower gait, for at long last the mystery which had encompassed him since his arrival in the Yellowstone country was beginning to make sense.

Also, he knew something Abel Poirer didn't know. The defunct Tom Smith, whose real name had been Ford Younger, was a sometime stage bandit. Ford had at one time run with a brace of other outlaws. The loner reached back in memory for the names of those other men, couldn't come up with them, and let that part of it go.

Ford Younger had been apprehended down near Raton after a savage chase, had been tried, convicted, and sent to territorial prison for three years. He'd been out of custody six months when the loner came across Ford Younger trying to break into the loner's line of work. In fact, Younger had twice suggested that they team up. Both times the loner had declined, and after the second time the association between those two had steadily deteriorated, until, a few nights previous, in a smoky saloon in Lincoln, their association had been permanently dissolved in a blaze of sudden gunfire.

The loner was running some other things together in his mind when Abel stepped up onto the porch-walk dead ahead, turned, and halted facing the loner. He unexpectedly said, "I'm sorry, Loner. I guess I did say more than I had to."

"Forget it," the loner exclaimed. "Let's get inside and see where all this is goin' to lead us."

Abel nodded, turned, and reached for the door latch.

TEN

The loner's reaction to meeting Antoinette Poirer was visible in the first long look he had at her. Even while her father was introducing them in the large, comfortable parlor of the main house, something confused and confusing entered the roundabout atmosphere. Nettie looked up from her chair at once, sensing this. Abel, in the act of unprecedented hospitality towards a common range rider—pouring two stiff drinks for himself and the loner—did not catch it at all.

Toni Poirer was tall. She had her mother's dark, liquid eyes and her father's strong build. She was in her mid-20s and very handsome. Her lips, with a soft heaviness, parted as a sudden break of interest shadowed her face when she stood up and looked straight at the loner. She nodded without speaking, never once looking away.

The loner's tough gaze gently widened, and his face changed. A gusty expression of surprise came and went. He'd obviously been too otherwise occupied with his thoughts to expect anything as abruptly startling as this lovely, willowy woman standing there ten feet from him.

Something flashed between those two, something entirely foreign to what had brought them together. Nettie felt it, and quick concern showed from her long, upward gaze at those two. Then Abel walked over, handed the loner a glass, and spoke to his daughter.

"Honey, tell him about the holdups."

The girl explained, and in essence, her words were little different from what her father had already said. But now and then there was a drag, a break, to her flow of words, as though something more insistent was struggling to hold her attention. Then she finished speaking, went to a chair, and dropped down.

The loner backed up to the fireplace. The heat striking against him was good. The liquor he'd downed added its warming substance, too. These things combined loosened the loner, not only in the body. His expression showed a softness none of the others had ever before seen in it, and if Abel overlooked this, neither Nettie nor her lovely daughter did. But that softness also had a hint of sadness in it.

Abel said, "Conway can verify everything Toni has told us, Loner. He can get in touch with the Denver authorities by telegraph."

"Yeah," murmured the loner, his gaze resting quietly upon Abel's daughter. "Maybe we're on the right trail and maybe not, but it comes to me now that I should've spent more time at Hennesey's saloon."

"We'll pay Hennesey a visit as soon as this storm lets up. I'd like to get a look at those two gunmen Conway told me he'd hired to act as bartenders."

This casual statement brought the loner's attention around. He stared a long time at Abel without saying anything.

"*Two* gunmen?" he ultimately and softly asked.

"Yes. Joe said something about them. He didn't attach any particular attention to them, only that Pat Hennesey wouldn't hire expensive gunfighters unless he—"

"Like I told you, Poirer," interrupted the loner. "Tom Smith ran with a tough pair of outlaws at one time. Those three specialized in robbing stages."

Abel looked at the loner, then down at the empty glass in his hand. He said, "It's beginning to appear that we just might be on the right track after all," he said. "Care for another drink?"

"No."

Abel turned to refill his own glass. Nettie, seeing how her daughter's dark gaze rarely left the loner, put aside her knitting and stood up.

"I'll make some coffee," she stated. "Come along, Toni, you can help me."

The loner ignored Abel as long as that tall, handsome

younger woman was in sight, but when she and her mother passed beyond view, he said, "Poirer, if Smith and those other two are the stage bandits, why would they be tied in with Hennesey?"

"Well," the wealthy rancher said, turning back with his re-filled glass in one hand, "why wouldn't they be tied in?"

"They wouldn't need a fourth man. Outlaws of their kind don't usually operate like that. They hold up their stages, divide the loot, and make themselves scarce. Their kind has no need for a saloonman who doesn't even ride with them."

"Maybe not," assented Poirer. "But we're getting ahead of ourselves. What we don't know is all the ramifications of this thing—providing that these are the same outlaws wanted down at Denver and over at Cheyenne."

This was true enough. The loner stepped away from the fireplace. He hadn't removed his sheepskin because he hadn't meant to stay this long at the main house, and it was getting warm.

Abel waved him to a chair. Clearly, Abel was not exclusively occupied by this affair, and clearly too, his several drinks had loosened Abel away from his customary coldness towards others.

"Ten thousand?" he said suddenly, facing the loner with his legs spread wide and his head lowered a little.

"Five thousand now, tonight, and five thousand more when you hand me those land patents. Fair enough, Loner?"

"We're discussing something else," said the loner coldly, and did not take that chair after all. It irritated him to believe Poirer was turning affable for a private reason; he'd never liked deviousness in people.

Abel smiled, his face a little flushed. "We'll get to the bottom of your attempted murder in a day or two, Loner, but the Yellowstone outfit's been around a long time and it will be around a long time to come—after this other thing's been forgotten, probably, so let's talk about the more important thing."

The loner's antagonism turned his face hard again. He crossed to where he'd put down his hat, scooped it up, and turned doorwards without a word. At that precise moment, though, Nettie and Toni Poirer returned with a tray and the coffee. Nettie, seeing the loner at the door, said, "Don't leave just yet, Mister Smith. Have some coffee first."

Abel, his affability abruptly gone, kept a cold gaze upon the loner. He twisted, put aside his empty glass, and afterwards helped his wife with the coffee tray. Over her father's bent back, Toni Poirer looked straight at the loner and quietly smiled.

"It's snowing out," she said. "Hot coffee tastes good on snowy nights, Mister Smith." She took a cup to her mother, got it filled, crossed over, and held it out.

The loner put aside his hat, took the cup, caught the fragrance of this beautiful woman's hair, caught the disturbing warmth of her closeness, and smiled back at her.

"I guess that wind has stopped," he said, neither thinking nor caring about that yonder wild night now. "I hadn't noticed."

He walked back with her to the table and filled a cup for her. Nettie, watching them with a worried, anxious expression, turned to Abel. She took up the conversation where it had lagged, in this manner diverting Abel's attention from something which was becoming increasingly apparent: their daughter's quick interest in the loner, and his reciprocal interest in their daughter.

Innocently, Nettie said to her husband, "I've heard it said over in Lincoln that Pat Hennesey has been forming a land syndicate."

Abel stared at his wife. Over beside Toni Poirer, the loner slowly turned and gazed at Nettie, too. Neither of them said anything for a while, and Nettie, seeing this quick, hard interest, looked slightly ruffled by it.

"Well, at the Ladies Aid last week, there was some talk of Mister Hennesey and several other men trying to get land options around town."

Abel's returned aloofness dissolved for the third time

this night. He swung his gaze over to the loner. "Out of the mouth of babes," he murmured. Then he said in a sharper manner, "Nettie, why didn't you tell me this before?"

"Abel, you never liked gossip."

"Gossip? But this isn't gossip, Nettie."

She shrugged a little apologetically. "Every time I've come home from a meeting of the Ladies Aid, you've grumbled at me for repeating the things I've heard, Abel. You know for a fact that you have."

The loner carefully set aside his half-emptied cup of coffee, straightened up, and said, "Mrs. Poirer, you didn't happen to hear who Hennesey's pardners were in this land syndicate, did you?"

"No, no one seemed to be clear about that, Mister Smith. Is it important?"

The loner gazed at Abel. "I thought you'd told her what we suspected," he exclaimed.

"I didn't mention Hennesey, if that's what you mean," Poirer replied.

The loner turned sardonic towards Poirer. "Now'd be a good time to do it," he dryly said. "Seems to me she's got as big a stake in this as you have, Poirer."

Abel's face reddened and his eyes turned yeasty towards the loner, but he didn't say anything right away, not until the loner murmured something to Toni, left her by the table, and went on over to retrieve his hat for the second time. Then Abel began to explain to his wife how Pat Hennesey was conceivably involved, not only in an effort to gain title to Yellowstone land, but also in this other thing which included the attempted murder of the loner.

As those two talked back and forth, their daughter went over to the loner. "It's still out," she murmured. "The stars are close enough to reach out and touch. I love nights like this one." She took down a cape that hung close by and handed it to him, turned for him to put the cape across her shoulders, faced back around, and said, "I'll go as far as the porch with you."

They passed out of the house, into the sharp, congealing cold beyond, and halted at once to gaze at those endless layers of falling snow, one behind the other for as far as visibility endured.

The stars were indeed seemingly close enough to reach forth and touch. They shone with a brightness seen at no other time of the year than in mid-winter. Altogether, the night was so deathly still and hushed that there might never have been a wild wind presaging this snowfall at all.

The loner halted at the overhang's edge. Beyond the porch at his feet was a virgin sifting of purest snow. Where starshine touched down, out across the yard, only two little squares of orange light shone—from over at the bunkhouse. Everywhere else, the cold night ruled indisputably.

Beside him, Toni said, "Mister Smith, have you ever stood in the falling snow and wondered if perhaps this wasn't nature's way of telling us there must always be a renewal, a freshening of life and promise and hope?"

He turned and looked down into her slightly uplifted, tilted face. She was very lovely in his sight, with soft starshine upon her cheeks, her creamy throat, her dark, rich hair.

She turned when he did not answer. They were standing close. He lowered his head tenderly and brushed her mouth with his lips. She did not draw back, and she afterwards smiled at him, as though in gratitude for the salute to her which this little kiss actually was.

"Thank you, Mister Smith. I'd have felt disappointed if you hadn't," she said, then turned to gaze outward again. "When I was a little girl, I didn't think there could be anything as wonderful, as peaceful and beautiful as this ranch." She paused, then looked out and around where snow was silently building up over weathered, old, sturdy buildings. "And now, since I've been away so long, I'm more sure than ever there is no comparable beauty in the world—at least not for me."

The loner also gazed out and around. For a long time, he simply stood like that. Then he slowly reached inside his sheepskin, drew forth a thick envelope, and handed it to her.

"For your father," he told her quietly. "But actually they aren't for him, Miss Toni—they're so that he'll be able to always keep this intact—this world you love."

The loner stepped out into the snow, moving away.

ELEVEN

To a man without purpose in life, fifteen thousand dollars, or ten thousand, or even five thousand, has less value than the look he might see in a beautiful woman's solemn eyes. The substantial things of life seem less permanent than the intransient things.

The loner pondered about this the following morning as he beat his way through a foot of flake-snow to the barn-lot, fed the horses, and did whatever chores he otherwise saw that needed doing. None of the other men at the bunkhouse were stirring yet. In fact, it was a little before five o'clock, and the loner was abroad for a specific reason. He meant to begin the long, cold ride back to Lincoln, now that the storm was over, and the prospect of saying goodbye held as little appeal for him as accepting Nettie Poirer's sympathy also held.

He rigged out the animal he'd ridden to Yellowstone, stepped up over cold leather, and rode quietly out across the ghostly white yard.

Against the frigid, far horizon, a sickle moon was set

slightly above some faint-standing peaks. Elsewhere, starshine shone with frosty whiteness over this endlessly silent, soft white world. The breath of both horse and rider steamed in the cold; there was a little rustling sound as the horse pushed along eastward, and the air was very dry.

The loner went past the Devil's Postpile, discerned that particular huge boulder behind which he and Abel Poirer had found the empty cache, saw also how those ageless stones wore their caps of flaky white, and swung to watch the sun make its valiant effort to penetrate a thick gray haziness over in the gunmetal east.

His ears began to ache, so he turned up the collar of his sheepskin. Later, when the bitter cold seeped inside both coat and gloves, he looped his reins and swung both arms against his body to stimulate sluggish circulation. There was a particular little ache where he'd been shot; it seemed to be linked between both those healing places. It didn't actually pain him. It was more like the dull aftermath of a light blow.

When the world eventually began to brighten, to turn pewter-colored in the steely dawn, the loner caught sight of dark, small squares far ahead where Lincoln hugged the plain. There were several sickly lights showing up there, but only a rare few chimneys and stovepipes gave off straight-standing thin spirals of smoke, and for another half hour the loner did not catch the good fragrance of pitch-pine burning, or the unmistakable odor of dry oak smokelessly giving off its traditional cherry-red heat.

He kept his gaze upon the town, but his thoughts were still back at Yellowstone. He thought only briefly of Poirer's purest astonishment at being handed those land patents which he so cherished, gained by him at no cost whatsoever. This was no longer important to him.

He'd meant for Poirer to have the land. That arguing over price had never been anything but a horse-trading ritual with him.

When he'd handed the papers to Toni Poirer, he'd been doing nothing particularly spontaneous. Even when he'd brushed her lips with his mouth, he hadn't been acting rashly, because the loner was not a mercurial type of man.

It had been when she'd told him what the Yellowstone meant to her, and it had also been the way she'd affected him with her smile and her wholesome, sturdy beauty.

He rocked along now, hunched down into his sheepskin, wondering how that had happened; he'd met a hundred handsome women since his wife had died. None had ever got past his reserve, even the ones who had tried hardest, and yet here, in the space of moments, when she had looked at him, it had been as though he'd never had any reserve at all. It was as though something was preordained between them.

After that meeting, everything else seemed trivial, seemed suddenly pointless and immaterial. That had been why he'd surrendered the land patents without even considering their value at all. She had said there was no place on earth as beautiful to her as Yellowstone, and he, feeling bound to her suddenly and irrevocably by something he did not understand at all, had suddenly felt that way, too. Had felt that Yellowstone should be kept inviolate for her. So, without a word or a second thought, he had made her a present of the legal papers which would keep her world safe for all time; the same papers for which one man had already died and other men would cheerfully kill to possess.

He had given away a fortune, and he didn't care one whit that this was irrefutably so, and yet, the knowledge of what he'd done made his face grave as he came down into Lincoln's main thoroughfare, passed Pat Hennesey's Lincoln Saloon, turned in at the livery barn and handed his animal into the care of a puffy-eyed hostler whose red cheeks indicated he'd just been pulled away from a stove somewhere.

There was a little activity in Lincoln now. That far-away horizon was still stubbornly resisting the sun's powerful efforts to shine through, but the roadway was lighter and on across the way, lamps were being lighted here and there as merchants prepared for the new day.

At one little café where steamy windows indicated someone had been at work making early breakfasts for some time, the loner saw a coated figure loom up from southward, pause to reach for the latch, and afterwards push on inside. He recognized that man's walk and his bearing, even though poor light under the opposite overhang prevented him from seeing the man's face. That had been Deputy Joe Conway, over there. The loner had ridden seventeen miles in congealing cold to talk to Joe, among others, so he struck out across the road for that same café.

It was like entering a new world, stepping into that café. The room was cheery with lamplight, it was wonderfully warm, and the sharp smell of cooking hot food struck the loner at once, bringing on a sudden awareness of hunger.

There were several other men at the counter, all bundled in coats, but Joe Conway was the only man there wearing the traditional sheepskin coat of rangemen. The others were townsmen of one kind or another.

The loner went over, straddled the bench beside Conway, sank down, and flung back his collar as he looked around.

"Good morning," he said, as the lawman looked at him. "You're an early riser."

"You seem to do a pretty good job at that yourself,"

Conway responded, showing civility but no friendliness. "I thought you'd left town, Smith."

"No. Poirer and I rode out to a place called Devil's Postpile on Yellowstone range. After that, we saw the storm coming and headed for his ranch. I spent the night there."

Conway had a thick crockery coffee cup enfolded in both hands. He sipped and sighed, looked around, and said, "You mean you rode in from Yellowstone this morning?"

"Yes."

"Why? Why ride seventeen miles before sunup, in the coldest time of day, Mister Smith?"

"To ask some questions."

"Of me?"

"You're one of the fellers I want to talk to, yes." The counterman brought Joe Conway's breakfast, raised his eyebrows at the loner, got another breakfast order, and padded away in his carpet slippers.

Conway continued to hold that warm cup between both hands for a while, making no move to start eating. "Did Mister Poirer ride in with you?" he eventually asked.

The loner shook his head. "For all I know, he may not even come to town. What I'm interested in, Deputy, concerns me directly, not Abel Poirer."

"All right, let's have it."

"You told Poirer about Hennesey hiring a pair of gunmen for bartenders."

"That's right."

"What are their names?"

Conway looked up. His face was saturnine. "Odd you should ask," he dryly said, "One's named Jones and the other one's named Johnson."

"No Smith?"

Conway smiled. "I guess the place was gettin' cluttered up with Smiths," he said.

"I'm going to tell you a little story," said the loner, and recited the tale he'd already told Abel Poirer about defunct Tom Smith and his two outlaw companions who'd been stage robbers.

Joe Conway still didn't touch his breakfast, but near the end of the loner's recital, he drained the coffee cup and set it aside.

"Yeah," he murmured. "I know about that." Then he looked into the loner's surprised face to shrug and go on quietly speaking. "Just because a feller's a hick-town deputy doesn't mean he's also got to be simple-minded, Smith."

The loner thought a moment, perceptibly nodded, and told Deputy Conway what Toni Poirer had related about the stage robberies between Denver and Cheyenne.

"Know about that too," said Conway, finally taking

up a fork and going to work on his food. "Let me do a little guessing too, Smith. You and Poirer got something in mind that makes you figure those Colorado outlaws and Hennesey's friends might have a connection. Right?"

"Right."

"Mind telling me what it is?"

"No," replied the loner, and told Conway of the cache he and Abel had discovered. He went on to explain how he'd been shot, and after that had happened, how he'd come to realize that in some way Tom Smith and Pat Hennesey were implicated, not only in his shooting, but also in some scheme to grab Yellowstone's free-graze range.

"Do you know," asked Conway quietly, "that Hennesey and his two gunfightin' friends have formed a land syndicate?"

"We know about the syndicate, but we didn't know who Hennesey's pardners in it were."

"Well, now you know."

The loner's breakfast came. Neither he nor Joe Conway said anything more for a while. They ate and thought and were silent until Conway pushed back his plate, leaned upon the counter, and motioned for a refill for his coffee cup.

"Mister Smith," Joe said, "I think maybe you an' Abel an' me had better meet at my office and have a little talk. You see, there are some things you fellers know which I need to know—and I know a few things you fellers ought to also know."

"Forget Poirer for now," answered the loner. "Like I told you—from here on this is my fight, not his."

But Deputy Conway shook his head over this, saying, "'Fraid it's not that simple. You see, one of the things you don't know is that Pat's been raising Cain about me refusing to hand over some land patents Tom Smith had in his possession when you killed him, and those claims have to do with Yellowstone range."

"Hennesey's got no interest in those claims, Conway."

"Well now," drawled the deputy, "it seems that he has. He came to my office yesterday—him and his two hired guns—and said he'd put up the money with which Tom Smith bought those papers. He even showed me a legal paper signed by Tom Smith saying Smith, Hennesey, Jones, and Johnson are pardners in the Lincoln Land and Homestead Company."

The loner twisted to stare at Conway.

The deputy gravely inclined his head. "It's a fact, Mister Smith. That pardnership paper was drawn up by a lawyer, and it's legal as all get-out."

"Did you give him the land patents?"

"No. I stalled him. You see, I'd already promised Mister Poirer I'd keep quiet about those patents— otherwise Hennesey'll advertise in eastern newspapers about cheap plough-land, and within two weeks we'll be overrun by squatters. But Mister Poirer's got to sit in on our talks; the way I see it, his interest in this mess is more important than your interest is. All you want is a crack at someone who bushwhacked you. But you survived that, Smith, and if Hennesey has his way, Poirer's Yellowstone outfit isn't going to survive at all."

Conway emptied his second cup of coffee, leaned forward to arise, and looked the loner squarely in the face. "I'll send a rider out to Yellowstone for Poirer," he said. "Meet me at my office in an hour or so. All right?"

The loner nodded, Conway stood up, stepped over the counter-bench, dropped several coins, and walked on out into the steely day.

The loner finished his breakfast, slowly coming to a realization that he'd made a bad mistake in underestimating both Pat Hennesey and Joe Conway. When he finished, paid for his breakfast, and stood up, the little café seemed fuller of townsmen than it had been when he'd entered earlier. Their voices rose in a hum around him, their red faces and heavy coats seeming to fill that small place. He pushed on out to the boardwalk where a little icy wind struck him, forcing him to momentarily catch his breath. He stood out there for a while watching Lincoln come to life in a sluggish way, turned finally, and went along to the hotel. There, he climbed to his roadside room, fired up the stove, heated water, and shaved.

It was his intention to go to Hennesey's saloon next. After that, he'd meet Deputy Conway at the jailhouse, but first and foremost in his mind was the wish to have a long look at Pat Hennesey, whom, it was beginning to solidly seem, was more than just a fat, sly saloonman, and was also some kind of an evil master-mind capable of operating a number of underhanded enterprises at once. Also, while the names Jones and Johnson palpably were false, the loner had seen wanted-poster-pictures of defunct Tom Smith's outlaw cronies and wished to ascertain now whether or not Hennesey's barmen were the same renegades.

TWELVE

The Lincoln Saloon lay diagonally opposite the livery barn. There were a number of similar establishments in town, but Hennesey's place seemed to be the favorite hangout for stockmen as well as a great number of townsmen.

It consisted of one long room with a bar running almost the entire length of the eastward back wall. Between the bar and spindle-doors facing the roadway were poker tables, chairs, and between the doors and a dirty glass window sat a battered old piano.

The room had a peculiar, endemic smell to it which seemed to have so thoroughly permeated even the woodwork that summer or winter Hennesey's saloon always smelt the same. That scent was a powerful compound of horse-sweat, man-sweat, whisky, and strong tobacco. It was not an offensive odor; at least, it didn't offend Hennesey's patrons—either townsmen, freighters, travelers passing through, or cattlemen— and when the loner stepped through those swinging doors, this odor did not offend him either. It was the same fragrance one found in just about every saloon west of the Missouri, north of the Canadian, and south of the Gallatin.

There were not many customers at Hennesey's place. It was much too early in the day for serious drinking, yet there was a poker game in progress in a far corner, near the wood-stove, and there was one patron over at the bar conversing desultorily with a hatchet-faced, swarthy bartender.

The loner took a long look at that barman as he strolled over, hooked both elbows upon the bar, and waited for the barman to come up where he was. There was no expression upon the loner's face; he might have been a passing traveler or a cowboy in from some outlying ranch, yet this blankness hid a surge of excitement, for the loner recognized that bartender. He was one of the wanted men Tom Smith had run with, the darkly sinister outlaw called 'Frank Lester' on the wanted posters. The name came back to the loner as he stood there watching that hatchet-faced man.

With deliberate casualness, the swarthy, thin-faced barman strolled over, lifted his eyebrows, and waited.

"Whisky," said the loner, "and a little information."

That cruel face turned hard. "We got the whisky, but I don't know about the information. What kind you lookin' for, cowboy?"

"I want a few words with Pat Hennesey."

"Do you?" said the barman softly, his black, bold gaze pushing against the loner. "What about?"

"None of your business," replied the loner in just as soft a tone.

Frank Lester stood completely still. He had one hand—the left—lying easy atop the bar. His right hand was out of sight below the bar. His bleak stare turned appraising, then his right elbow moved the slightest bit.

"Don't do it," said the loner, still speaking so softly that none of the others in that room had any inkling all was not well. "Just stand easy and you'll live a little longer—Frank."

The barman's eyes drew out narrow in a long, careful study of the loner's face, but his right arm stopped moving.

"Who are you, mister?" he asked.

"That's none of your business either. Go get Hennesey. Tell him there's a man out here wants a few words with him."

Frank Lester did not move right away. He seemed to be considering several courses of action. The loner comprehended this.

"You'd better move," he told the barman. "I'll bat my eyes just once, and if you're still standing here afterwards, I'll yank a little slack out of you."

"Yeah?" breathed the cruel-eyed man.

"Yeah!" answered the loner.

Lester turned very quietly and started down the bar towards a small, dark door with the word "Private" lettered upon it in thick black letters. He entered, down there, and emerged a moment later with two other men.

The loner recognized the leaner of those two at once as Tom Smith's other former running-mate, Lorenzo Simpson, called Simpy by his acquaintances, but known here in Lincoln as Johnson.

The largest of those three was unmistakably Pat Hennesey. He was heavily paunched and waddled when he walked, but if this might have provoked humor, a second glance would have stilled any thoughts of Hennesey being amusing. His eyes were small, close-set, and like chips of pale blue ice. He had a massive jaw and a bloodless slit for a mouth.

Now, as he led those others up towards the loner, Hennesey's appearance was far from amusing—it was unmistakably threatening and sinister.

Hennesey stopped across the bar and glowered. He said nothing, his unwavering stare silky-soft and deadly as he waited. Behind him, Frank Lester and lanky, sleepy-eyed-looking Lorenzo Simpson stood back waiting and watching, their attention riveted upon the loner. No one would ever mistake the lethalness of those three, and neither did the loner.

He said, "Hennesey, you weren't here the other night

when Tom Smith got killed, were you?"

Hennesey still said nothing. He only shook his head.

"That's too bad, because if you had been, you'd recognize me. I'm the man who killed him."

Hennesey's eyes sprang wide open. The two gunmen behind him also showed clear surprise. When Hennesey opened his mouth to speak, the tallest and leanest of those three cut across Hennesey's forming words with a sharp comment of his own.

"You're Cole Flynn," he said. "They know you hereabouts as Bill Smith—and the loner."

"And you," replied the loner, "are known as Johnson, I take it. But your name actually is Lorenzo Simpson. You an' Frank Lester there were old friends of Tom Smith's." The loner's voice was dryly sarcastic. "Old friends in a lot of ways, Simp."

Hennesey stared hard at the loner. In a growling, low mumble, he said, "So you're Cole Flynn. I've heard a lot about you."

The loner left off watching the other two men. He raised his eyebrows at Hennesey. "That makes us even. I've heard a lot about you, too."

Hennesey seemed uncertain of his ground. He said, "Flynn, Tom told us about those land patents you have. We need them."

"I reckon you do at that," stated the loner dryly. "Tom was working for you all the time, and I never even suspected he had a friend until after I'd killed him. Hennesey, I'll hand it to you—you're smart."

Hennesey seemed pleased by this praise. He relaxed a little, hitched at his belt, and leaned across the bar. "Tom was stupid, Flynn. He was supposed to get you to throw in with him in this deal I'm organizin'. Instead, he got you mad and got himself killed." Flynn smiled. "But maybe things work for the best. With him gone, we got an opening for another man in our syndicate."

"I'll bet you have, Hennesey, but you'll want me to put in those land patents."

"What's wrong with that? Hell, Flynn, we all stand to make a fortune."

"That's possible," agreed the loner. "But there's something else I want settled first."

"Name it," said Hennesey, warming to this conversation.

"I want the name of the man who shot me out at the Devil's Postpile on Yellowstone range, and I want to know why he did that."

Hennesey drummed lightly atop the bar with his right hand for a long moment. He tried to see past the loner's flinty, expressionless face and didn't succeed, so he eventually stopped drumming, straightened up, and shrugged.

"Tom Smith shot you," he said. "That take care of your question?"

"Not quite. He's dead, and you're probably lying."

Hennesey's face darkened. "You got a bad habit of bein' pretty free an' easy with your mouth," he said.

The loner nodded, giving Hennesey glare for glare. "I've got an even worse habit, Hennesey: I shoot first and fast." For a second, none of those four men scarcely breathed, then the loner spoke again.

"But let's say you're telling the truth, that Tom Smith really did shoot me. Now tell me why he did that, Hennesey?"

"I don't think I'll do that," said the fat saloon owner.

The loner put his head slightly to one side. He said, "Well, I'll make you a little bet, fat man. You'll start talkin' in the next five seconds or I'll bet you my life I can put two slugs through your head and one each into Frank and Simp back there, before any one of you can get your guns unlimbered."

Hennesey, Lester, and Simpson were like stone. Around them, the saloon's only noises were tinkling poker chips over by the wood-stove and dripping snow-water from the overhead roof.

Finally, Hennesey said, "Tom warned us about you, Flynn. He said you were trouble in spades to what we've got going."

"So you sent him out to bushwhack me."

"No, he told us that afterwards."

"I see, so now you want to take me up on that bet?"

Hennesey shook his head. He was less than five feet away and as large as he was, Hennesey knew perfectly well that whether Frank or Simp got the loner, the loner was sure to put those two bullets through his head first. No matter who afterwards won that wager, Hennesey knew he was going to be the loser, so he shook his head and said, "No bet, Loner. I sent Tom out to dig up something we had hid at Devil's Postpile. You see, he'd told me you had the patent on that particular piece of Yellowstone's range an' I couldn't take any chances on you peddlin' it before I got my cache emptied."

"That," stated the loner, "is the first thing you've so far said that I happen to know is the truth, fat man. Now tell me what was in that cache."

"Sure," said Hennesey, but at once both Frank Lester and Lorenzo Simpson voiced vigorous protests. Hennesey held up a pudgy hand to silence those two, and he coldly smiled at the loner.

"Sure, I'll tell you—the minute you hand me those Yellowstone land patents you have, I'll let you in on everything. I'll make you an equal pardner along with Simp and Frank."

The loner met the cold gleam of crafty confidence in Hennesey's little pig-eyes with a bitter little smile of his own. "You're about to lose a bet," he murmured. "I asked you a question, Hennesey, and you'd better answer it straight out—what was in that cache?"

Hennesey shifted his weight and gently wagged his head. "I'm not going to lose the bet," he said. "Loner, did you ever shoot a man in the back?"

The loner made no reply to this.

Hennesey's porcine features creased into an oily smile, and he started to turn away. "You're goin' to have to shoot me in the back now, if you want to make good that threat of yours," he said, and started to slowly walk back down the way he'd come. He padded past both Lorenzo Simpson and Frank Lester, presenting his thick, quivering back to the loner. He kept right on going until he got back down where the little office door was, and there Hennesey walked on out of sight without once looking back.

The loner watched Hennesey's retreat to its definite conclusion. He then swung his gaze back to the gunmen. "He runs a good bluff, boys. For a pig of a man, he runs a good bluff."

"Doesn't he, though?" murmured lanky Lorenzo Simpson. "I'm wonderin' if you can run one too, Flynn?"

"I know how you can find out, Simp. Come on out from behind that bar."

Simpson didn't move. Slightly behind him and a few feet farther south, Frank Lester carefully raised both hands, placed them atop the bar, and leaned there. He made a small, triumphant smile.

"You're holdin' a busted flush," he said to the loner.

"You come in here fired up for trouble, an' now you got to walk out with your tail between your legs. Aren't either Simp or me goin' to draw on you, Loner."

"No," drawled the loner. "I didn't expect you boys to. Not face-to-face anyway. But from here on out, I'll be right careful about passing across the mouths of dark alleys."

"You do that, Loner. And I'll give you some more advice too—stay out of Hennesey's saloon and stay out of our way on the range too."

The loner shifted his gaze back to lank Lorenzo Simpson. "Of the three of you, I'll make a guess," he said. "Simp, you're the only one that's got the guts to fight a man in a stand-up shoot-out. If I'm right, then keep a sharp eye peeled because Frank and that tub of lard down there in his office will scheme some way to get you into a shoot-out, and Simp, the day that happens—you're goin' to get killed."

The loner stood on for a moment longer, gauging those two. He had no doubt at all that the moment he turned his back, Frank Lester would willingly try a back-shot.

"Put your guns on the bar," he said.

Simpson tensed. "Go to hell," he whispered.

The loner's pistol barrel appeared, just the tip of it, over the bartop. "I said put 'em on the bartop." He cocked his weapon.

Both Simpson and Lester shucked their weapons, Frank indifferently, but Simpson with a coldly furious look. The loner holstered his own weapon, picked up those other guns, and walked on across the room. As he was passing through the doors, he dropped the six-guns and walked on out.

THIRTEEN

Abel Poirer rode into town in the middle of the day with his Yellowstone crew. The lot of them were armed to the teeth, and as they walked their horses down Lincoln's main thoroughfare, each man had his coat hanging open, his holstered .45 visible, and his right hand lying easy.

But nothing happened. A lanky, drowsy-eyed man lounging outside Hennesey's bar looked those riders over carefully and afterwards sauntered back into the saloon. This was Lorenzo Simpson, but neither Abel nor any of his men knew Simpson, so, while they noticed that casual retreat, they attached no great significance to it.

The townsmen recognized Abel. They also recognized his Yellowstone men, but since Abel rarely ever came to town without some kind of an escort, the townsmen paid no particular attention to the riders now as they went about their business.

Abel put in at the livery barn. Afterwards, while he

waited for his men to come out, he stood there upon the plank walk looking over the town.

It was slightly warmer at midday than it had been hours earlier when the loner had arrived in Lincoln, but it was still too cold for loiterers to be standing around. Roadway traffic was not as heavy as it ordinarily was either. Run-off snow-water made little corrugations in the roadway mud, and the sound of this melting snow was the one constant sound. Otherwise, Lincoln was relatively quiet.

Over at the buggy works, a steady dark cloud rose straight up into the thin air from a smokestack. At the hotel, there were straight-standing spirals of smoke, too.

Vern Patton came up and halted beside his employer. Behind Vern came old Puma and Martin Caine. The last two Yellowstone men to hike out of the livery barn were young Drew Ruddabaugh and yeasty John Landon. John had his sheepskin tucked under his shell-belt, permitting a clean and uninterrupted sweep downward for his right hand towards that ivory-butted .45 he wore. Landon looked as though he expected trouble at any moment. So did the others, but Landon seemed most willing to face it.

Abel turned without a word and started southward towards the jailhouse. As he and his riders passed grimly along, it began to strike the few townsmen who were also outside in the cold that something was wrong.

Several of these men came together across the road to watch Abel and his men push on into Joe Conway's office. There was a little flurry of excited speculation. Afterwards, those townsmen fanned out to hasten along, to pass the word and stir a rumor to life. Abel Poirer was in town with his whole crew; every man-jack was armed and grim-faced, they had all entered Conway's office, and it looked like bad trouble.

Even Deputy Conway, who was drinking coffee with the loner when Abel entered, sensed the willingness of these men to make trouble. For once, old Puma Partridge wasn't saying a word, which in itself presaged something unusual. Joe gestured towards a dented, grimy big pot over on the stove. There was a crudely nailed wooden shelf above the stove holding a row of chipped cups.

"Help yourselves," Joe said.

Everyone but Abel trooped across to get some of that simmering coffee. Abel pushed back his old hat, ran a look from the loner on over to Conway at his desk, tugged off his gauntlets, and pushed them carelessly into a coat pocket.

"I got your summons," he told Conway.

"I see you did," replied the lawman dryly. "I see you also read more into it than I intended." Joe made a backward gesture towards the Yellowstone men crowding up to the stove. "Came loaded for bear, Mister Poirer."

"I had my reasons," stated Abel, turned, and put a quiet gaze upon the loner. "I owe you some money, Loner. I brought that with me, too."

"You owe me nothing, Poirer," answered the loner from his tilted-back chair. He was hatless and coatless. It was warm in the little jailhouse. "I made you a present of those patents."

"You don't owe me anything, Loner."

"I didn't do that because I felt beholden. I did that because by rights, in my sight anyway, that damned land is already yours."

"Is that the only reason?" Poirer softly asked, his gaze cooling towards the loner. "My wife has an idea there was more to it."

"Your wife, Poirer, is one in a million," the loner said softly. He paused, looked skeptically at the rich cowman, then said in the same quiet way, "Don't look a gift horse in the mouth."

These two might have continued fencing with one another except that Joe Conway, sensing something between them and wishing to avoid a split at this crucial time, broke in.

Joe said, "Mister Poirer, I've got a positive identification on those two gunmen Hennesey's hired as barmen. The loner knows them." Conway shuffled through untidy papers atop his desk, picked up two wanted posters, and held them out to Poirer. "Here are their pictures and their records. These are old posters, a couple years old in fact, and I'd forgotten ever receivin' 'em. But when the loner gave me the names of Frank Lester and Lorenzo Simpson, I dug 'em up."

Poirer took the posters and studied them. While he was doing this, the loner told of his earlier encounter with Hennesey and those wanted men in the Lincoln Saloon. Conway spoke, too, explaining all that he and the loner had pieced together. It made a very damning case against Hennesey, Simpson, and Lester.

Abel put down the posters, crossed to a chair, and sat down. Over by the stove, his men were standing quietly, watching those men near Conway's desk and carefully listening to all they said back and forth.

"Then it was that Tom Smith who shot you," said Abel to the loner.

For an answer, he got a little shrug. "Maybe. He'd have done it, I know that for a fact," the loner stated. "But he's dead, I'm recovered, so it doesn't really matter now. It also could've been either Frank or Simp, but like I said, that's past now and done with."

"Then," said Poirer with quiet emphasis, "your part in this is finished, Loner."

Conway and the loner turned to stare. Abel met those surprised looks with a dogged insistence. "All he wanted was to square up with whoever shot him," Abel told the deputy. "And now that's been done, so he can stay out of the rest of this."

Conway turned his head a little to silently consider the loner. He was clearly puzzled by this sudden change. He seemed to be rummaging for a reason for it.

The loner made a wry face. "I never drop out of a game until it's finished," he said to Abel. "All the same, I thank you for your protective interest."

"It's not my protective interest," muttered Poirer, still staring straight at Joe Conway and avoiding the loner's speculative gaze.

Conway, with no knowledge of anything but what had happened in his town, looked more puzzled than ever. But the loner sat there on his tilted-back chair, steadily regarding Abel Poirer.

Finally, the loner said, "No? Am I allowed to ask whose protective interest is involved, Mister Poirer?"

"You don't have to ask, Loner. You already know."

The loner's chair came down off the wall with a sharp crash. He looked at Joe Conway, at the Yellowstone men across the office behind Joe, then he stood up, reached for his sheepskin, and said, "Well, I'm in this up to my ears, boys, and I aim to go whole-hog, so forget about me droppin' out. All the same, Abel, I'm grateful."

Abel was staring at his big hands. He said nothing, and Conway began to sputter.

"Say what the hell's goin' on here? Listen, you two, if there's something else I should know—"

"It's not your affair," broke in the loner quietly. "Forget it, Joe. Just concentrate on this other thing—this trouble with Hennesey and his pardners."

Conway swung towards Poirer. The cowman somberly nodded his head up and down in grave agreement with the loner. Those two had very effectively closed Conway out. He recognized this and acceded to it, although he certainly did not propose to forget about it; when this Hennesey trouble was taken care of, Joe meant to return to this other affair and get to the bottom of it.

The loner said to Abel, "The remaining land patents to your range are in Conway's safe. You can take them over, and that will end your range problems. The details are simple enough; the way most big cow outfits work is to register each claim in a rider's name, make the legal improvements, prove-up, and then change the title from your rider's name into your own name. Usually, fifty dollars in gold satisfies your riders."

Abel leaned back and nodded. "With the claims you gave Toni last night," he said, "that'll secure Yellowstone's range."

"Right." The loner faced Conway. "Open the safe. Joe, give him the papers."

Conway was turning in his chair when Poirer said, "Whoa up there." He shot the loner a cold stare. "Are you trying to edge me out of this fight that's coming up?"

"What've you got to fight about?" demanded the loner. "You only wanted to protect Yellowstone. All right, it's as secure as the law can make it. So you can take your boys and head for home."

Now Joe Conway spoke up, and Joe was prickly with swift anger. "Dammit all, you two," he exclaimed. "I got no idea what's between you, but first, Mister Poirer doesn't want the loner hurt, and now the loner doesn't want Abel Poirer hurt. Confound it, you two, I thought this was our combined fight. If you fellers both drop out, I'm left with my head stickin' up a mile high for Hennesey to shoot at."

"I told you I was stayin'," said the loner. "There're only three of them, Joe. You and I can handle that."

"Three that you know of," put in Abel Poirer quickly. "Loner, you don't know Pat Hennesey as well as Conway, and I know him. He's probably bought himself another three local gun-punks. That's how Hennesey operates." Abel stood up. "Joe, I'm staying, too."

The deputy swung around, squinted over at Abel's Yellowstone riders, saw those blank, watchful faces, and swung back again. He wagged his head dolorously. "Someone tell me something—just what the hell are these two tryin' so hard to protect each other for, an' just ten minutes ago they were lookin' icicles at one another."

Over at the stove, old Puma cleared his throat as though to speak. Instantly, Vern Patton's bony elbow somehow got wedged painfully between two of old Puma's ribs on the left side, and John Landon's elbow cut him hard under the ribs on the right side. Puma gasped, winced, and slammed his lips closed. At that same moment, the loner spoke again.

"All right," he said briskly. "Here are the facts as Joe and I have put them together about Hennesey and his friends. First off, those two bartenders over there at the saloon aren't named Jones and Johnson; they're named Frank Lester and Lorenzo Simpson. They're professional outlaws who specialize in hitting stage coaches. We're pretty certain they are the men who've been raiding stages between Denver and Cheyenne. We'll know about that when Conway gets an answer to the telegram he sent to the Denver police while we were waitin' around for you Yellowstone men this morning.

"Next," continued the loner, "we believe Hennesey's using that stolen money to set up a big land deal involving not just the Yellowstone range, but other land as well. If he's the mastermind behind those stage robberies, he's got the men to do this with, but even more important, he's been gettin' the holdup money as well to finance this land deal with."

Abel Poirer's eyes widened slightly, but he said nothing. Obviously, Poirer had never once suspected the magnitude of this scheme of Hennesey's, and now, as he listened, comprehension and amazement both were reflected in his expression.

"One thing stumped us," went on the loner. "That cache out at Devil's Postpile. We still may be wrong, too, but what it looks like now is that, since some of the stage loot wasn't cash money, and was actually gold ingots that're easily identifiable, Hennesey didn't want them hidden at his saloon where he could never give an alibi for them."

"I'll be damned," blurted out Abel. "Of course. Toni said some of that stage loot was gold bullion. You've hit it on the head, Loner."

Joe Conway, though, wagged an upraised hand at Poirer. "This is all guesswork," he cautioned. "Unless we find that gold, Mister Poirer—find where they've re-hidden it—we'll likely never be able to tie the three of them to those robberies at all, and so far we've got nothing but hunches to go on."

The loner said, "It's the hunches we're going to have to run our bluff with, Poirer. Joe can arrest Lester and Simpson because they're wanted men. But if neither of them talks, there's not a blessed thing he can arrest Pat Hennesey for."

Abel looked at the lawman thoughtfully for a moment before saying, "He's smart, Conway. I always thought he was crooked, but I've been underestimating him. He's set this thing up so that no matter who else gets hurt, he'll be in the clear. Why else hide the gold bullion fifteen miles from here out on my range? So if anyone ever accidentally stumbled onto it, they'd think a Yellowstone rider was involved."

The loner looked wryly over at old Puma Partridge. "Hennesey almost achieved that," he said, "with me, and I didn't even suspect there was any stolen gold hidden on Yellowstone range."

Joe Conway got up, went after his coat, and said, "All right, we're goin' after those three." As he shrugged into the sheepskin, he looked around. "Vern, you and the others separate after we leave here, but don't come with Mister Poirer an' the loner an' me. Split up and keep an eye on Hennesey's saloon. Stay out in the roadway. If there's shootin', you boys keep those three from escapin' out of town,"

Vern started to protest. So did hot-tempered John Landon with his right hand lightly lying upon the ivory handle of his .45.

But Joe Conway was adamant. "Listen, boys," he said. "If the bunch of us walked in up there, hell would bust loose for sure. I want those men alive if it can possibly be done that way."

Joe carefully tucked his coat under his shell-belt on the right side, took up his hat, and dropped it carelessly upon the back of his head. Across from him, the loner was also donning his coat and hat. Nothing more was said until the three leaders crossed over to the door and hesitated. Then Conway looked into the faces of all those men who were crowding around him.

"Good luck," he murmured, and reached for the doorlatch.

Outside, the sun was beginning to drop off westerly, a freshness was making that feeble warmth lose its heat as cold late afternoon closed down, and Lincoln's slushy roadway shone with bright little twinkling frozen places.

FOURTEEN

The loner led out across the road. Behind him came Abel Poirer, and the last man to leave the jailhouse side of the road was Deputy Conway. Joe waited to make certain Vern Patton and his Yellowstone men would not follow. They didn't; each cowboy sauntered along the near plank walk, remaining on that westerly side of the road.

There was very little activity elsewhere upon the boardwalks. The sun was turning red, its heat was gone, and most townspeople were staying indoors. The overhead sky was crystal clear. This presaged a bitterly cold night to come.

The loner paused upon the opposite plank walk, let Poirer come up even, and said, "Just a minute, Abel. There's something I've got to say before I walk into that saloon, and I'm not very good at sayin' things like this. In fact, it's been so long since I've tried that I'm havin' trouble just rememberin' the right words."

Abel stood there regarding the loner with solemn

eyes. He thought he knew what was coming, but he made no effort to help the loner with his particular dilemma. Abel just stood there and waited.

The loner glanced towards Hennesey's saloon, then out into the roadway where Deputy Conway was slogging his way through ankle-deep mud towards them. He drew in a big breath.

"Abel, it's about your daughter."

"I thought it would be," murmured the cowman, his face woodenly unreadable.

"Well… I don't know how to say it."

"Maybe," said Abel coldly, "I'd better just pay you the fifteen thousand dollars for those land patents."

The loner's face slowly paled. His eyes grew dark. "Are you intimatin' that I tried to buy your approval of me callin' on her with those damned papers, Abel? Because if you are, I'm going to knock your head off for that."

"Do you believe you could do it?"

The loner snorted, "With one hand tied behind me," he exclaimed.

Those two were glaring when Joe Conway finally came up to them, paused and kicked big clods of wet mud off his boots, turned and opened his mouth to speak, saw their white, savage looks, and stood there dumbfounded for nearly ten seconds before he finally spoke.

"Damn it," he snarled at Poirer and the loner. "Listen to me, you two idiots, I've had about all this private feudin' I figure to put up with. One minute you're tryin' to protect each other, the next minute you're set to tear out each other's throats. By gawd, I'm through humorin' you two. Now, we're goin' after Hennesey, and if either of you so much as look sideways at the other again, I'll whip the pair of you to a fare-thee-well."

Joe took a long step up, got between Poirer and the loner, glared at each man in turn, looked on across the road where the Yellowstone riders had taken their watchful positions, turned, and with each hand gave his companions a rough forward shove.

"Let's go," he growled. "You want to fight, you two, just save it for another five minutes an' you might get all the battlin' you want at the Lincoln Saloon!"

The three of them resumed their onward way. The loner's face was still pale with wrath, but he put his entire attention forward, upon the yonder saloon, and did not so much as glance from the corner of his eye at Abel Poirer again.

It abruptly occurred to the loner as he paced along that Lincoln was not just seemingly devoid of pedestrians because of the increasing cold. He saw faces watching them through store windows as they swung past. He commented on this to Conway. Joe looked around, shrugged, and said, "Funny thing about rumors: they spread faster'n the telegraph when it's a matter of getting word around."

Up at the hitchrack before Hennesey's place, several humped-up horses patiently stood, but in front of the doors themselves, there wasn't a single loafer standing around. The loner also noticed this and sniffed to himself about it. Their coming was not entirely unexpected, he thought.

Just before the three of them swung to enter Hennesey's bar, Joe Conway took two long forward steps and hit the doors first. The loner and Abel Poirer entered the place three feet behind Joe.

There were a number of men idling at the bar. These turned at the rough entrance Conway made, registered slow surprise at the expression Joe was wearing, and turned to stone where they stood.

There were several cowhands playing seven-up over in the gloomy corner near the stove. These men also twisted to gaze doorward, and the same thing happened here; those men, entirely ignorant of what was in process but guessing at once from the entrance of Conway and his companions that trouble was afoot, became motionless and wary-eyed.

The bartender, in the act of making a long swipe across the bartop with a damp rag, stopped in mid-motion, watched Deputy Conway cross towards him, and very gradually got both feet squarely under him, forgetting about that rag he was wielding.

Joe halted just short of the bar. "Where's Hennesey?" he demanded.

The barman lifted his shoulders and dropped them. "Dunno," he mumbled.

"You better make a real good guess," said Joe, beginning to scowl.

"Ain't seen him since about two hours back, Joe," said the disturbed barman. "I relieved that new feller. Him and Pat went off with Johnson. I got no idea where they went, Joe, honest. They just got on their horses and went ridin' northward out of town. I seen 'em go past the window. That's all I can tell you."

Conway seemed to lose some of his spring-tightness. He turned to run a slow look around into all those watching faces, saw no one he particularly wished to see, and halted, facing Abel and the loner.

"Dry run," he muttered, and added a fierce swear word to that.

The loner, though, gently wagged his head at Conway. "Maybe not," he said in a tone too low for others to hear. "You got the right to look through Hennesey's office, or do you need some kind of a legal paper, Joe?"

Conway squinted up his eyes. "What you got in mind?" he demanded.

"There's bound to be something around here that'll incriminate Hennesey. Him not bein' here just might be a blessin' in disguise. You said yourself you didn't have any grounds to arrest him. Let's see if we can't find some grounds."

Conway thought on this through a quiet interval while those spectators in the saloon kept silently watchful. Finally, he nodded.

"Good idea. Come on, we'll start with his office."

The three of them were advancing upon that little gloomy door marked "Private" when the barman hastened down to intercept them. He said to Conway, "Joe, you can't go in there. That's Pat's office an' he's left strict orders whenever he's not here for none of us to let anyone in there."

Conway brushed the barman aside. "You want to spend six months in jail for interferin' with a law officer in the authorized performance of his duties?" he said.

The barman hung back muttering little squeaky protests, but he did not again attempt to bar the way of Conway, Abel Poirer, and the loner, as those three barged on into Pat Hennesey's dingy, small office.

Poirer closed the door and leaned upon it, letting his eyes become accustomed to the gloom of this foul-smelling, cluttered room, which, because it lacked windows, was nearly as dark by day as it ordinarily was by night. The loner stumbled over something in the middle of the room and swore. Joe Conway found a lamp, lit it, and held it high so they could all see around them.

There was an immense steel safe in one corner, which was the largest single piece of furniture in Hennesey's office, larger even than the roll-top desk which stood solidly against the rear wall. Conway went over to ponder that massive safe. Abel Poirer remained where he was by the door. The loner stepped over to Hennesey's desk, tried the roll-top, found it locked, picked up a knife from a little table, and inserted it, pried, and broke the roll-top loose. He slid the thing up and began rummaging through drawers and pigeonholes.

For a while, none of them had anything to say to one another. It was Conway, turning away from the safe, who ultimately broke that silence by commenting on the impregnability of that laminated steel box. He also said he'd bet a new hat there was incriminating evidence in there, but that it might just as well be on the moon.

The loner, with a little scrap of paper in his hand, turned to gaze over at Joe. "Maybe this'll help," he said, and went over to hold that scrap of paper close to the lamp for Conway to read.

"What is it?" Poirer asked from over by the door.

"A list of currency furnished to Tom Smith over the past eight months," answered the loner. "And I'd say from the total amount that Hennesey's put up the cash to ruin a lot of cowmen by havin' Smith buy land patents to free-graze range."

Conway took the paper, thoughtfully folded it, put

it into a shirt pocket, and said, "But it doesn't say what that money was advanced for, boys. All Pat's got to do is deny he gave that money to Smith to buy land patents with; all he's got to do is say those were wages."

"Pretty high wages," commented the loner.

Conway agreed with that, but said the paper was not incriminating enough. He and the loner went over to the desk and resumed searching.

They found several deeds to land parcels east of Lincoln. They also found four land patents without names upon them whose legal descriptions the loner recognized as belonging to distant areas of the Yellowstone range. When Joe wasn't looking, the loner pocketed these.

In the end, they found nothing which would seriously incriminate Pat Hennesey, and when the lawman made a dour comment about this, Abel Poirer told him they shouldn't be disappointed, really, because Hennesey had amply demonstrated that he was a crafty as well as a cold-blooded man.

The loner stepped across to also gaze at that tantalizing strong-box, but he went a little further than Joe Conway had done; he walked from one side of the thing to the other side, leaning close to examine the seams as well as the huge external tumbler to the combination lock. It was when he leaned upon the rear wall and casually looked into the little dark, narrow place between wall and safe that he saw something. He drew forth his pocketknife, worked this thing partially loose, put up the knife, caught hold of soiled, rough cloth, and tugged. Out came a mud-stained and knife-ripped canvas bag.

Joe Conway let out a grunt and sprang over to snatch the bag away from the loner, shake a big cloud of dust from it, and hold the thing aloft where they could all see it.

Abel Poirer gave a little startled cry from over by the door, he could see the reverse side of that bag. "Turn it around," he breathlessly ordered Conway. "Look at the printing on the front of the thing."

Conway obeyed. Both he and the loner saw that faded, discolored lettering. It was the name of a Denver, Colorado, bank.

Joe went over to Hennesey's desk chair and dropped limply down. He stared from Poirer to the loner, then at the bank pouch he was gripping in both hands.

The loner said dryly, "Incriminatin' enough, Deputy?"

Conway nodded and puckered his eyes. "Loner, I'm grateful. If you hadn't been so all-fired snoopy, we'd have gone out of here barehanded. Someone stuffed this thing back there and forgot about it after slashin' it to take the money out."

"Then let's get out of here," said Poirer. "And Joe, stuff that bag inside your shirt. If Hennesey's barman sees you with that thing, he'll tell Pat—then the fat'll be in the fire. Now, come on, we got what we came for."

Conway stood up, dutifully stuffed the bank pouch under his shirt, and followed the others out of Hennesey's office.

FIFTEEN

Nearly all the patrons of the Lincoln Saloon had disappeared from that outer main room by the time Joe Conway and his companions emerged from Pat Hennesey's office. At the bar, that same sour-faced and disapproving man was mopping at the counter-top, but aside from him, only two other men remained in the place. Both these men seemed to the loner to look less than impartial. Both were rough-looking range-hands, scarred, grizzled, and capable-seeming. They considered Poirer, Conway, and the loner with hostile eyes. None of these men said a word until Conway was twisting to throw his shoulder against the spindle-doors. Then one of them growled in a rumbling tone at Joe.

"Find anything, lawman?" That dark and villainous range rider asked Conway. "Pat'll want to know."

Conway turned, gazed steadily at that cowboy, and said, "If Pat's interested enough, he knows where my office is."

The barman drew courage from the range rider's careless hostility and said, "Deputy, Pat'll have your badge for what you done in here tonight. You had no right to search this place."

"We could argue that," said Conway. "I've got that right any time." He pushed one of the doors open and let in a fiercely cold rush of air.

"I didn't see no search warrant, Deputy."

"You didn't ask to see one," said Joe, and passed on out of the saloon.

The other hard customer at the bar turned to study Poirer and the loner. This man wore a perpetual sneer, but no one would ever mistake that sneer for a bluff. This man not only wore his six-gun tied down, but he also had four visible notches carefully carved in the hard-rubber grip. He was a killer.

This man addressed the loner, saying, "Mister, you just bit off a heap more'n you can chew, bustin' in here like you an' your friends done."

The loner carefully faced back around towards this man. "You'd be surprised how much I can chew," he said softly. "Maybe you'd like to find out."

Now the atmosphere became suddenly clearer. Now the previous fencing had given way to a definite challenge.

The barman started to step back, to withdraw his visible hands from the bartop. Abel Poirer said, "Don't try it, barkeep. You reach under that bar and it'll be the last reach you ever make."

Joe Conway came pushing back inside again, his face pinched up into a quizzical expression. In one glance, Joe saw what was in process. He dropped his right hand to within inches of his .45.

"So Pat didn't take all his friends out of town with him," Joe said. "That's interestin."

Conway said no more. None of the others spoke either. The crushing silence drew out to its maximum limit, then that other rangehand on across the room let his shoulders slump.

He said, "Forget it, Nevada," to the man with the notched gun. "Let Pat handle it."

The rough customer called Nevada did not immediately relinquish his opposition, though he continued to stand there with his hostile stare upon the loner.

"You just got some good advice," said Joe Conway to Nevada. "If I were in your boots, I'd take it."

Very slowly and sneeringly, Nevada turned his broad back upon those men over by the door, leaned with both elbows upon the bar, and growled at the bartender. "Gimme a shot," he said distinctly, "to wash the taste of them three out'n my mouth."

Conway waited this time until Poirer and the loner walked on out before he exited from Hennesey's saloon for the second time.

Out upon the boardwalk, the three of them paused for just a moment. None of them spoke, but each of them looked over to where the Yellowstone men were idly keeping their vigil. Finally, Conway jerked his head and started southward, back the way they had come. Across the road, those Yellowstone men interpreted this move to mean they, too, should converge upon the jailhouse. They also turned to pace along southward.

When Conway, the loner, and Abel Poirer stepped down into roadway mud opposite the jailhouse, a man behind them came out of a little tan-painted building waving a yellow paper and calling.

"Hey, Joe, it came back," this man said excitedly.

Conway turned and, without a look or a word, paced back, took the little paper, read it, then hiked on over to join the others in front of his jailhouse. He said nothing about the paper until they were all inside again and the door was closed. Then he handed it to the loner, waved a hand towards the simmering coffeepot, and led the Yellowstone riders over for something hot.

The loner passed that telegram to Abel Poirer. Poirer read it, looked over where Joe was sipping coffee, and said, "I never thought of that, Conway."

Joe shrugged. "There are usually witnesses to stage robberies, Mister Poirer, unless it's a massacre."

"How long will it take for them to get here from

Denver with that Denver policeman?"

Another shrug. "Tomorrow afternoon, maybe, if they make all the right connections and if the snow doesn't pile up between here and there in the meantime."

The loner strolled over, accepted a cup of java from young Drew Ruddabaugh, cupped his cold hands around the cup, and saw old Puma, Caine, John Landon, and Drew watching him.

"It's the answer to Conway's telegram to Denver," the loner explained. "It says Frank Lester and Lorenzo Simpson were identified as the stage bandits by passengers. That a Denver officer is comin' to Lincoln with two witnesses to identify Simpson and Lester."

The loner swung toward Conway. "Joe," he said, "show them that bank pouch."

Conway set down his cup, fished around inside his woolen shirt, drew forth the crumpled canvas bag with its unmistakable knife slash, and carelessly tossed it to Puma Partridge. He afterwards walked on back to his desk, sat down, drew up a legal form of some kind, and began writing.

"Warrant for arrest?" asked Poirer.

"Nope," replied the deputy. "The search warrant I should've had when we busted into Hennesey's office."

The loner and Abel Poirer exchanged a wry smile.

That bank pouch went the rounds of the Yellowstone men before Martin Caine strolled on over to drop it upon Conway's desk and return to the stove area where benign heat worked its wonders upon tired, cold bodies.

Deputy Conway finished filling out his search warrant and went to work filling out another legal form. "This one," he informed the others, "is a warrant of arrest for Pat Hennesey for suspected complicity."

"For what?" asked old Puma.

Conway turned and put a scowling look on the old cowboy. He turned back and went on writing. He didn't explain what complicity meant until he'd finished with that first arrest warrant and began filling out another one.

"For complicity, Puma, you ignorant old devil," he exclaimed. "Complicity means he's suspected of havin' a hand in illegal doings."

"Well hell," scoffed old Puma, "why don't you just write that down on your paper 'stead of confusin' folks with words they never heard of."

Drew Ruddabaugh laughed. Even dour and swarthy Martin Caine faintly smiled. Martin left the others, strolled over to Abel, and said, "Maybe one of us ought to sort of stand around outside, Mister Poirer, so's we'll know when Hennesey rides back into town."

Without looking around or giving Poirer a chance to reply to this, Joe Conway said, "That's a right good notion, Martin. Are you volunteerin'?"

"I reckon."

"Then go on," said Conway, tossing down his pen and swiveling around. "But stay out of sight because two minutes after Hennesey rides in, he'll hear about us rummagin' his office and he'll know we're after him for sure. I wouldn't put it past him to turn his gun crew loose on us."

Caine was nodding and moving towards the door as he buttoned his coat against the evening cold when the loner said something which caused all of them, Martin Caine included, to pause at whatever they were doing.

"I've been wondering just what was so important that it took fat Pat Hennesey as well as Frank Lester and Lorenzo Simpson out of town on a bitterly cold day like this."

Abel Poirer twisted where he stood to put a speculative gaze upon the loner. So did Joe Conway and the Yellowstone men.

"We've about decided that Hennesey was afraid to have that stolen gold bullion in his saloon. We're pretty sure he had it cached out at Devil's Postpile. Was in fact moving it when I stumbled onto someone diggin' it up an' got shot. What we don't know is where it was taken after I rode into that gunfire."

"Ahhh," breathed old Puma Partridge, comprehension filling his mind. "They went out today to dig it up again. It'd have to be somethin' that important to get Pat Hennesey to go ridin' out in weather like this. Ain't a man in this room that doesn't know how Pat hates to ride horses or leave his saloon."

Joe Conway struck one balled fist atop his desk. "I think you've got somethin'," he said to the loner. "Dammit, we should've ridden out huntin' those fellers after we left the saloon. You should've come up with this sooner, Loner."

"I thought of it sooner," stated the loner. "I also thought of something else, Joe: Why risk being seen by Hennesey or Lester or Simpson, trailing them, when if we sit comfortably around here where it's warm until they get back, we may find the bullion without buckin' the cold?"

Abel Poirer spoke up. "You mean you think Hennesey'll fetch the gold back to town to hide it?"

The loner spread his hands palms downward. "I don't know what Hennesey figures to do with that gold. All I can say is that he'll have to send it somewhere to sell it and get cash money for it. If we aren't fortunate enough to sweat it out of him where it's hidden, then we're going to have to watch him day and night until he or Lester or Simpson tries to ship it out of town."

Poirer thought a moment, then said swiftly. "Listen, if there's a gunfight, we can't kill those men. If we do, no one'll ever find that gold."

Conway nodded over this. He swiveled for a look at Ruddabaugh, old Puma, and yeasty John Landon. "You heard that," he warned the Yellowstone men. "For gosh sakes, don't kill 'em."

Drew and old Puma Partridge nodded, but John Landon didn't. John said wryly, "Deputy, I respect gold as much as the next man. But I sure never figured it was worth gettin' killed for, 'thout tryin' my damnedest to kill whoever was after my neck over the stuff."

The loner said: "Shoot low, Landon, if it comes to shooting." This admonition sounded testy; the loner was annoyed by the narrowness of Landon's view and showed it. Landon subsided, the loner went to a chair and was in the act of dropping down, when the roadside door opened, swarthy Martin Caine stepped in, and the loner did not complete his bend towards the rearward chair after catching one glance at Caine's face.

"They just rode in," pronounced Caine. "Right now they're up at the livery barn."

Joe Conway stood up, reached for his hat, and dropped it atop his head. The men over by the stove put aside their coffee cups and stirred a little, milled around as though awaiting orders.

Abel Poirer, who had removed his sheepskin, began now to put the coat back on.

The loner said, addressing Caine, "Did they have anything with them, Martin?"

"Nothing that I noticed," replied Caine. "Just their saddlebags is all. No bullion box, if that's what you mean."

The loner pursed his lips and faintly frowned. He'd hoped against hope that Hennesey would have returned with the stolen gold.

Caine spoke again. This time, his words turned every man in that little office perfectly still and staring. He said, "Just before them three rode in, Miz' Poirer and Miz' Toni drove in up at the livery barn too."

Abel looked suddenly stricken. "What?" he demanded. "Are you positive about that?"

"Yes, sir, Mister Poirer, I'm plumb positive."

Abel looked helplessly at the others. "I don't understand," he muttered. "Why would they come to town in the evening like this—in the coldest part of the day?"

Old Puma, trying to be helpful, said, "Maybe something's wrong out at the ranch, Mister Poirer."

Vern Patton shot Puma a look. So did Drew Ruddabaugh. Puma lapsed into total silence, offering nothing more and looking abashed for having said that much.

Conway scratched his nose and gazed steadily at Abel. Finally, he said quietly, "Mister Poirer, you better go get your women under cover over at the hotel. This isn't goin' to be any picnic, when Hennesey finds out we're closin' in on him."

The loner agreed with this by nodding his head. Abel gradually collected himself, controlled his astonishment, and went on over to the door. As he swung that panel open, he said, "Wait here for me. I won't be long."

Sure," said the lawman. "We'll wait. But make it as fast as you can because while we're willin' to wait, I got a feelin' Hennesey won't be so willing."

Poirer passed out into the bitterly cold and gloomy dusk, closed the door after himself, and hurried away.

SIXTEEN

Joe Conway's admonition to Abel Poirer proved correct. Abel hadn't been gone from the jailhouse more than ten minutes when a solid sound of approaching booted feet carried on to the men inside Conway's office, and a moment later, the roadside door was violently opened.

Pat Hennesey filled that opening with his bulk and his cold fury. Behind him were other men. From where the loner stood off to one side, he could see at least two rugged faces out there in the descending night; they belonged to those two rangehands he and Conway had exchanged words with at the saloon an hour before.

Hennesey made no move to come on inside but remained planted in the doorway with frigid air rushing in around him. He had a thick blanket-coat hanging upon him, which added to his normal massive bulk, making him seem even larger than he was.

He glared over at Joe, where Conway was standing with his back to the shotgun rack. "What d'you mean, bustin' into my office?" he demanded in a tone choked with wrath. "Who the hell d'you think you are, Conway? I'll make you eat that tin star you're wearin' for that."

Joe, bracing into that solid anger, seemed to the loner to be turning cold, turning efficiently ready for whatever was going to happen.

He said, "Hennesey, I've got a warrant for your arrest. You an' Lester an' Simpson."

"You have, have you? Well, you two-bit punk, let's see you try an' serve it. Who d'you think you are anyway, tryin' to frame me'n my pardners with some silly charge of law-breakin'?"

The loner moved, drawing all those eyes to him. He went across to the desk, picked up that slashed bank pouch, and held it for Pat Hennesey to see.

"It was stuffed down behind your safe," the loner quietly stated. "I reckon you forgot it was there, Hennesey. It's from a Denver bank."

Hennesey's eyes jumped to that canvas bag. Just for a second, they showed total surprise. Then they blanked over, turning fiery again. "Prove that," he snarled at the loner. "Just try an' prove that, Flynn. I figured you for a troublemaker. I should've turned Simp and Frank loose on you when you tried playin' the big wheel in my saloon this mornin'. Well, it's not too late for that yet." Hennesey waved a contemptuous hand at that bank pouch. "You figurin' on arrestin' me for that thing, Conway?" he snarled. "Forget it if you are. I never seen that pouch before in my life."

"It was in your office, Hennesey."

"Yeah?" growled the fat man. "You got witnesses?"

"Sure," said Conway. "The loner and Abel Poirer."

Hennesey smirked. "Not good enough, Conway. All I got to swear to in court is that I never saw that thing before, and I got cause to believe you three fellers brought it with you an' planted it in my office so's you could trump up this arrest charge."

"Tell that to a jury," said Joe, still with his back to the shotgun rack. "Don't tell it to me, Pat, because I'm goin' to arrest you anyway."

From behind the fat man, the rangehand called Nevada stepped up, pushed a double-barrel shotgun through, and said, "Try it, lawman. Take one step towards Hennesey. Go ahead—just one step."

The loner tensed. From the edge of his vision, he saw the Yellowstone men over by the stove stiffen. John Landon and Vern Patton, in the forefront, had their right arms slightly hooked upwards, their fingers within inches of their holstered guns.

"Go ahead," Nevada taunted those completely exposed men under the pitiless lamplight of Conway's little office. "Go ahead, someone, just give me half a reason to turn this thing loose in that room. You boys ever see what a shotgun does among bunched-up men in a small room? It's a sight to see."

"Hennesey," said the loner. "Tell him to withdraw that gun."

The saloonman swiveled little pig's eyes from Conway to the loner. He made a bitter, cruel little smile at the loner.

"You talked tough enough in my saloon this mornin'," Hennesey said, losing a little of his indignation and seeming to replace it with bitter pleasure now. "What happened to your guts, Flynn? Did they drain out through the soles of your boots?"

The loner stood staring at Pat Hennesey for a moment before answering, and his expression was exactly as it had been at their earlier meeting: Pitiless and deadly.

"You're a fool," he told the saloonman. "Sure, that scatter gun'll raise hell with us in here. But Hennesey, that big belly of yours is a beautiful target, and before that shotgun gets all of us, you'll be too dead to care. Now for the last time, Hennesey—*tell that man to withdraw that gun!*"

No one who heard the loner's voice would ever have misunderstood the solid promise of unleashed violence in it. Hennesey didn't make that mistake either. He glowered, but his cruel, small smile faded and his small, treacherous eyes grew very still, very speculative.

"Take the gun away, Nevada," he finally ordered, speaking quietly.

The shotgun was withdrawn. From behind fat Pat

Hennesey, someone muttered profanely. Joe Conway's voice cut across that mumbling out there upon the plank walk.

Joe said: "Pat, if you resist arrest, you're only goin' to make it harder on yourself."

"On you, not on me," snarled the saloonman. "Conway, you're not man enough to arrest me."

The loner dropped that canvas pouch, strolled back across where he'd been standing before Nevada pushed that riot gun into the room, and faced Hennesey.

"On all of us," he said to Hennesey. "You'll make it hard on all of us, Hennesey, but don't ever believe you're not goin' to be arrested. You an' Frank and Simp."

The saloonman stood there braced and bull-like, his dissipated, greasy face lowered a little as though he meant to charge the loner, drop his head still more, and lunge across the room.

"Come an' try it," he said. "Just you come an' try to arrest me. Any of you. That goes for you Yellowstone men, too, over there by the stove. Yellow is right. Poirer an' his *rough-tough* Yellowstone crew." Hennesey uttered a fierce curse. "Ought to leave the 'stone' out of that name an' just call Poirer's outfit the 'Yellow ranch.'"

The loner saw dark Martin Caine and testy John Landon settle cloudy stares upon Hennesey. He spoke up quickly to avert whatever those two might do or say. Hennesey had the upper hand here; the loner wanted to avoid a shoot-out until the lot of them could get out of this little lighted room.

"All right," he shot at Hennesey. "You've made your point. You're tough as nails and hard as iron, Hennesey. You want to try an' add anything to that? Because if you do, you'll be the second man to fall. One of us might be the first, but you'll sure as hell be the second."

Hennesey uttered another fighting insult, drew his mouth down at its outer corners, and said, "Conway, if you ever bust into my place again, I'll have you killed. You better believe that. The same goes if you ever try to arrest me, too—or arrest anyone workin' for me. And Conway, I got the kind of money to import the best gunfighters in the West. Now, you remember that and keep out of my way."

Hennesey stepped back, bumped into a man behind him, growled at that moving obstacle, reached ahead for the office door, and slammed it closed, hard, hiding himself and his gun-crew from sight of the stiff-standing men inside Joe Conway's office.

For a few seconds, no one said a word or moved. Finally, though, Deputy Conway slumped over where he stood, scowled at the floor, and shuffled over to his desk, where he perched upon a desk corner.

Vern Patton said something, but no one heeded it because John Landon let off a string of savage words. He gazed over at the loner. "I reckon you played it right," he said bitterly, "but me—I'd have called him."

"Sure," growled Conway, "and got us all perforated. No, the loner did what should've been done." Something seemed suddenly to occur to Joe. He raised his head, looked over, and said, "Flynn? Is that your real name, Loner?"

"Yes. Cole Flynn."

All those faces turned to carefully consider the loner. This was a delicate moment, though, and not a man among them had any comment to make.

Conway got off his desk, walked over, and took down a shotgun from the wall-rack. With his back to the others, he said, "Help yourselves, boys. These things, as you've just seen, are mighty handy weapons for backin' down a whole roomful of men."

At last, the Yellowstone men broke up, moved over to help themselves to the shotguns, and afterwards to also help themselves to the boxes of scattergun shells that Conway broke open upon a table. This is what all of them were doing with the solitary exception of the loner, when Abel Poirer walked in out of the freezing night.

They glanced up at Abel, but again, none of them had anything to say. The loner drew out his .45, spun the cylinder, examined the loads, dropped the thing back into its holster, and nodded over at the wall-rack to Poirer.

"Help yourself," he said. "Hennesey was in here a few minutes back and left a challenge for us to make good on Joe's promise to arrest him."

Poirer turned towards the lawman. "That's right," stated Joe. "That's how it happened. He backed the lot of us down with a shotgun, Mister Poirer."

Abel nodded, seemingly only passably interested in this warlike preparation. He walked over to confront the loner, raised a gloved fist, and held it out. The loner looked at that closed hand, put forth his own hand, and Poirer dropped something into it without saying a word.

It was a little gold locket in the shape of a heart. There were initials engraved upon the face of the locket which the loner tried mightily to decipher.

"Whoa," he murmured to Poirer. "Whose initials are these?"

Poirer said quietly, "Look inside," and walked on across to get a shotgun.

The loner found the locket's snap, opened it, and held the tiny, delicately painted picture to the light. A breath-taking likeness of Antoinette Poirer wistfully smiled out at him. He very gently closed the locket, held it tightly in his closed fist for a moment, then went over to tap Abel upon the shoulder, jerk his head, and lead Poirer beyond earshot of the others.

"Explain," he said.

Abel looked glum. "She wanted you to have it."

"Why?"

Abel raised troubled eyes to the loner's face. "First," he said, "let me tell you something. I've never before had a serious argument with my daughter."

"You had one tonight?"

"Yes."

"Over me?"

Abel inclined his head. "It was her insistence that brought them to town. She feared you and I might be killed if bad trouble broke out here between Yellowstone and Pat Hennesey."

"I see," murmured the loner. "Listen, Abel, I'm sorry about that argument. I didn't mean to come between you and Toni."

Abel did what was for him an unprecedented thing. He brought up a hand and let it lightly lie upon the loner's shoulder, then almost at once withdrew it.

"I know," he said quietly. "I guess I knew about the other, too. That's why I didn't want you to get involved. I didn't want to believe Toni was in love with you. I reckon my wife and I just didn't think it could legitimately happen so fast. After all, you two only met last night, Loner."

"Sure, Abel. I didn't think it could happen like that either. In fact, to be truthful, I didn't believe it could ever happen to me again. You see, I lost an awfully good woman, an' I reckon when she died somethin' went out of me. It's been a long time, Abel. I've been a loner ever since. Last night…"

"Yes?"

"Maybe we shouldn't talk about it. Maybe Toni's right: someone's sure to get hurt tonight. Maybe if we just don't say any more, it'll be better. That way, there'll be no sadness afterwards if something happens."

Abel shook his head. "There'll be sadness, Loner." He tapped the hand clutching the little gold locket. "I know my girl. When she asked me to give you that, it wasn't just out of pity for whatever might happen to you tonight. She sent her heart and her love with it." Abel paused, looked around the room, and back again. He made a gentle little smile. "Go ahead, get it off your chest," he said.

"I tried to tell you this once before, Abel, before we went into Hennesey's saloon. You were mad."

"Well, I apologize for that. Try to understand what something like this does to a father."

"Sure. Abel, since last night, I haven't been able to imagine any kind of a future without Toni."

"Loner, she has a little son. I guess you knew that, didn't you?"

"I knew it. My wife and I—well—we wanted kids. It just never worked out for us."

Abel pushed out his ungloved right hand. Those two

solemnly shook hands, then Abel asked a question. "Tell me something, why were you tryin' to keep me out of the fight today?"

"I guess for the same reason you tried to keep me out."

They smiled and strongly shook.

SEVENTEEN

Joe Conway, making a great deal of noise clearing his throat, broke up that little private talk across the room. Joe said, "All right, boys. Hennesey made his grandstand play. Now it's our turn." He squinted around. "You ready?"

Martin Caine said something unprintable about Pat Hennesey. "Called us the yellow outfit," he said. "I figure he's got to eat those words."

John Landon nodded grim agreement with this. Even young Ruddabaugh and Vern Patton looked grim, but it was old Puma who crowned those threatening comments when he said, "Been enough talk around here lately. Let's up'n *do* somethin' for a change."

Joe squinted at old Puma and nodded. "We're goin' to do something, boys. We're going to seal off the saloon and take Hennesey and his pardners all together or one at a time." Joe paused, made sure every man was watching him, then said, "Puma, you take the livery barn. Stay out of sight in there. Whatever happens, don't show yourself, and don't let anyone saddle a horse and ride out."

"Anyone?"

"Anyone! We don't know how many friends Hennesey has in town, or whether he has some beyond town. So you make blessed sure no one rides out for help. Particularly, if anyone tries runnin' into the barn from the saloon, don't let him get away. You understand?"

Puma understood and profanely said so.

Conway looked at Martin Caine and Vern Patton. "You two get around behind the saloon. Seal the place off from the back alley. Don't let anyone out or in."

Vern and dark Martin Caine nodded.

"John," said the lawman to Landon, "you stay with me. You an' I'll call on Hennesey to come out."

"Which he won't do," stated John Landon dryly.

"Then you an' I'll open the game," retorted Conway. "But accordin' to the law we've got to give him that chance."

Landon shrugged. He appeared neither reluctant nor enthusiastic.

"Loner," said Joe, "you and Mister Poirer keep on this side of the road, but go northward, above the saloon, and don't do anything until I give the word. If they mean to make a fight of it, though, you two keep 'em pinned down in there. All right?"

Abel nodded, but the loner faintly frowned at

Conway. "What've you got in mind?" he asked. "Listen, Joe, don't try and rush the place."

Conway started for the door. He shook his head at the loner, saying, "I'm not that stupid, but remember, this is my town. I know every crevice of it, and that goes for Pat Hennesey's building, along with the rest of the buildings here."

That was all Conway would say. He led the bunch of them out into the quiet, bitterly cold night and stood a moment looking up the roadway where Hennesey's hitchrack was full of tied saddle animals. As though in reply to the silent thoughts around him, Joe said, "Cowhands in from the ranches for some poker and a few drinks. They'll leave that place like a herd of scalded cats when trouble starts, and that's what you fellers got to watch real close about. Make blessed certain Lester or Simpson or Hennesey don't try rushin' out too."

Conway waved his free arm, made a peremptory gesture with it, and the Yellowstone men immediately broke away, heading for their allocated positions in pairs. Just before Abel and the loner started northward through the cold darkness, Conway turned and said, "If anything happens to me, you two are in command."

For a long time after those men broke up, there was nothing to be heard from them, and in fact, when several riders strolled out of the Lincoln Saloon to stand briefly assessing the nighttime sky and commenting back and forth on how cold they expected it to get this night, these were the only men in sight around Hennesey's place.

Abel and the loner were well northward. Behind them were several buildings, but mostly, the town lay south of where they ultimately halted near a recessed doorway.

As they watched those cowboys go down to their horses, the loner said, "Conway's up to something. He didn't make that remark about knowing his town just for the hell of it. He's got some plan in mind."

Abel, holding one of those jailhouse scatterguns, stamped his booted feet; it was bitterly cold. "Sometimes it takes something like this to make a man know his acquaintances better," he said to the loner. "I guess I've known Joe Conway for six, seven years. Now and then, I've bailed out my riders when they've gotten too big a load on at one of the saloons. But really, I've never known Conway. Not until today."

The loner turned, considered Abel, and said, "Well, if you like what you've seen so far, you could show it a little by calling him Joe instead of just Conway."

Abel looked sharply at the loner, but his companion, after saying this, was facing southward towards the saloon again, and if Abel meant to make a retort, he didn't get the chance. Deputy Conway's unmistakable bull-bass roar sounded through the brittle night air.

"Everybody in the Lincoln Saloon—clear out of there!"

For a few seconds after Conway had roared that order, the piano at Hennesey's place kept right on playing. Then it stopped. The other sounds of revelry inside also died out. A long, deepening stillness came to settle over that lamp-lighted place.

"Out!" Conway roared again. "You rangehands—get out of there. This is Deputy Conway speaking. Pat Hennesey is under arrest. Two men in there with him are also under arrest." Conway paused, then cried out again, this time in an altered tone. "Hennesey, come out and fetch Lester and Simpson with you. Your saloon is surrounded. Come out empty-handed. You've got five seconds!"

Suddenly, the loner saw those spindle-doors at the Lincoln Saloon quiver under the impact of pushing bodies. Townsmen and cowboys came thrusting out of the building in a rush. Some made straight for the hitchrack, others less collected, simply flung away in long-legged lopes heading north and south along the plank walk.

The loner stepped out into the roadway with his coat open, his six-gun-butt handy, and strained to make out the faces of the men rushing northward. Abel also came out into the roadway to do this. Southward, other men appeared out of dark places to slow that headlong rush of men and also seek to identify the faces streaming past.

For two or three minutes, while this mass exodus was in progress, the only sound was made by pounding feet. But as those hastening shadows diminished, Joe Conway called out once more, this time repeating his former order to Hennesey, Lester, and Simpson.

The loner did not believe Conway would be obeyed, and he wasn't. But Joe got a reply of sorts from Hennesey's saloon. Someone smashed window-glass with a gun-muzzle, aimed in the general southward direction of Joe's voice, and fired off a defiant shot.

This sudden gunfire cleared the roadway as if by magic. Some of the men who had left Hennesey's place had hurried only far enough away to feel safe and had then turned around to see what this was all about. That solitary wild gunshot inspired these bold spirits to renewed alacrity, only this time they ran into the byways leading off the main thoroughfare, leaving the roadway to Conway and his henchmen.

A second gunshot erupted suddenly, then a third and fourth. As the loner and Abel retreated into the dark protection of their recessed doorway, the loner said, "From around back. Hennesey or some of his friends must've tried getting out that way."

Abel, thinking of the men Conway had detailed to guard the saloon's rear, said dryly, "Martin Caine's not afraid of the devil himself. Neither is Vern. I wouldn't want to be Hennesey and try to get past those two."

The loner put out a hand, brushed Abel's arm with it, and pointed overhead. "Up there on Hennesey's roof," he said softly. "Watch for a silhouette up there."

While those two raised their eyes, Joe Conway called out again. But this time Joe offered Hennesey no truce; he explained how the saloon was completely sealed off and warned the men in there with Hennesey that they could not hope to survive if they persisted in trying to shoot their way clear.

As before, Joe's reply was gunfire. While this swelling, flashing bedlam was increasing as Conway's men began to return Hennesey's leaden defiance, the loner and Abel Poirer kept their overhead vigil.

They saw that shifting shadow again, but it dropped down when the roadside shooting increased. They kept watch, though, and eventually saw a rifle barrel glide over wood up there.

Abel raised his shotgun. The loner gently pushed it aside. "Range is too great," he said, drew his .45, and cocked it.

At the livery barn, someone with a six-gun was systematically splintering Hennesey's swinging doors with a .45. The loner thought he knew who that was, down there. He also thought old Puma was the target that overhead rifleman was trying to line up over his sights. He stepped out of the doorway, stepped almost to the edge of the plank walk, raised his handgun, and waited. A thick set of shoulders craftily appeared as that overhead rifleman curled close around his weapon, ready to fire. Down at the livery barn, old Puma was still firing.

The loner took a long bead, squeezed his trigger, and the red lash of his six-gun muzzle lit up the area where he stood for a blinding second. Someone inside the saloon immediately swung a rifle and fired in the loner's direction. It was a wild shot, didn't come very close, but it drove the loner away. As he backed off, he watched that overhead sniper raise up stiffly using both arms as levers, hang for a moment like that, then give a big shudder and sag over the roofline. The man's body slid forward, teetered briefly, then oozed downward. It fell heavily upon the rickety overhang which shaded those spindle-doors, rolled loosely to the edge of the overhang, and tumbled straight down into the roadway at the edge of Hennesey's plank walk. There, the dead sniper lay face-up with saloon lamp light falling across him.

Someone inside the saloon bawled out in astonishment at the sight of that dropping body, and afterwards, recognizing the dead man, cried out again. But the gunfire was building up again so that neither the loner nor Abel Poirer could make out those ripped-out words.

Puma's persistence finally paid off; one saloon door broke loose and crashed inward. This permitted Abel and the loner to see inside the room. Abel walked straight out into the roadway, threw up his shotgun, and let off a blast of whistling slugs.

Inside, someone squawked. The loner went out where Abel was, fired his handgun empty, reloaded, and winced when Abel fired off his second barrel. This time, the slugs tore loose the remaining spindle-door, lifted it under violent impact, and hurled it all the way back against the bar.

The defenders, split up in there, some of them on the right of the doorway, some on the left, seemed acutely disconcerted. Their gunfire dwindled. Even the occasional shots they threw outward had no targets.

Southwards, Joe Conway appeared, also out in the roadway's center. With Joe was yeasty John Landon. Those two also emptied shotguns into the saloon through that doorless, wide opening.

The saloon was utterly dark now. Some dogged defender at the broken northern window beside the piano stood his ground. This man appeared to be the only battler in Hennesey's place willing to face the increasing force of shotguns lining up out there in the roadway. He fired at Conway, shifted his .45, and fired the next time at Abel Poirer.

The loner tried three times to nail this man, failed each time, and was stepping sideways to minimize the other man's chances of a hit, when three shotguns, all trained upon the broken window, erupted simultaneously. The destruction inside Hennesey's place made by this solid blast of lead was audible even over the sounds of gunfire. Wood splintered, bottles broke into fragments, lamps exploded, and the building quivered.

Whoever had been firing from that shattered window did not fire again.

The loner grabbed Abel's arm and yanked him away. Abel had not moved since coming recklessly out into the roadway. There was no more gunfire coming from the saloon, but the loner was sure, even including that terrific blast of shotgun fire seconds before, that Hennesey's crew was not annihilated.

He led the cowman southward towards a juncture with Landon and Deputy Conway. They made it, but under the circumstances, this was not the wisest thing to attempt, and Joe growled something to this effect at them as they came up. The loner released Abel, ignored Conway's acid remark, and said, "Give them another chance to quit, Joe. We've got to get one of them out of there alive."

Conway, instead of complying, raised his shotgun, aimed in the general direction of the Hennesey's southernmost window, and fired off one barrel, staggered, cocked his second barrel, and blasted off with that one too. As he was reloading, he said, "We already got one of 'em. But Pat's still in there—him an' Frank Lester—and I want them too—one way or the other."

The loner and Abel stared at Conway. Abel pushed up, brushed the lawman's scattergun aside, and said, "You already got one of them—how, Joe?"

"I told you I know my town, didn't I?" growled the lawman. "I got down into Hennesey's attic by a skylight. When a feller came upstairs to climb onto the roof, I caught him, disarmed him, and brought him down the back of the cussed building. Vern and Martin Caine gave me a hand down with him. They also threw some lead through the rear wall to keep Hennesey from interferin.'"

Abel's jaw sagged. The loner said, "Which one, Joe?"

"Simpson. But it was danged close, Loner. Another one was comin' up even as I was shoving Simpson out the skylight. I caught a quick look at that one."

"Yeah," said the loner. "The one they called Nevada."

Conway nodded. "How'd you know?"

The loner didn't answer. He turned to gaze over at Hennesey's wrecked saloon, and at the dead man lying over there.

There seemed now to be only one man firing back at Conway's attackers. He seldom fired twice from the same place, which is probably all that kept him alive because everyone except Martin Caine and Vern Patton, who were behind the building, was now boldly firing from out in the intensely cold and wetly starlighted roadway.

The loner turned back. "Give the fool a chance," he called over all that savage gunfire to Conway. "He couldn't surrender if he wanted to, Joe, with everyone firin' at him."

Conway reluctantly lowered his shotgun, nodded at the loner, and bawled out for the firing to stop. It did, almost at once. Silence settled, drew out ominously, then Joe called on the solitary survivor from Hennesey's saloon to walk out. He did, with both hands stiffly raised, hatless, shuffle-footed, and looking dazed. It was Frank Lester.

EIGHTEEN

The loner walked over where Lester had halted upon the boardwalk's edge to stand gazing at the dead man lying face-up over there.

"Nevada," said the loner to Lester. "He was on the roof."

Just as conversationally, but in a voice slightly thick and dragging, Frank Lester said, "Yeah, him and Simp went up there."

"Simp's a prisoner."

Lester, still with his rigid arms high overhead, lifted his gaze to the loner's face. "Simp—captured?" he said, seeming dazed.

The loner nodded. He said, "Where's Hennesey?"

"Inside. He was crossin' the room when that big shotgun blast come. It fair cut him in two."

"And that other one, the feller who ran with Nevada?"

"Caught one square between the eyes while he was kneelin' beside me at the window."

"You're lucky, Frank."

Lester, watching the crowd of men walking forward with Deputy Conway, numbly nodded his head. "Lucky," he repeated, then dropped his eyes to the loner again and said in a slightly stronger voice, "Hell, was Pat ever wrong. He said that deputy sheriff an' you other fellers didn't have enough sand in your craws to try an' clean us out. Man alive, was Pat ever wrong."

The loner stepped past Lester as Joe Conway came up with Abel and the others. He walked on into the wrecked saloon, saw a crouching man at a broken window who seemed to have slumped down in deep sleep. This was the rough-looking rangehand who had been Nevada's partner.

Across the room, directly in front of the bar and also directly in line with that same shattered window, lay fat Pat Hennesey. Pat was on his stomach, face down. Frank Lester hadn't exaggerated; Hennesey had been riddled by shotgun slugs.

The room was a gory shambles. The loner gazed around a moment, then went back out into the cold night, where Vern Patton and Martin Caine were just joining the others.

Here and there up and down the roadway, men were gingerly, tentatively, stepping out into sight. A few bold spirits were starting forward where Deputy Conway had Frank Lester in tow and was herding him down towards the jailhouse.

Occasionally, someone called out to those heavily armed men in the roadway, from over upon the boardwalks, but there were very few answers to these questions as the Yellowstone men hiked along behind Abel Poirer and Joe Conway.

The loner was the last of those attackers to leave Hennesey's place. He strolled down the southward plank walk quietly and unobtrusively. He passed excited townsmen who didn't recognize him, got all the way to the hotel doorway without being accosted, and was halted there in mid-stride by a soft, inquiring voice.

Toni Poirer stepped out, her face lifted, her eyes dark-ringed, and her heavy mouth lying parted in a questioning way.

The loner halted, gazed straight at her a moment, then rummaged inside his coat, brought forth several papers, and handed them to her. "I'm all right," he said. "So is your paw. Here, put these papers with the other ones I gave you. They came from Hennesey's office. More land patents to Yellowstone range."

He would have moved on then, but she stopped him with a soft touch upon one arm. "Don't go," she whispered.

He turned back. The fight was still a smoky light in his eyes. His hatbrim-shadowed features looked gray and drained dry. "I'll be back," he told her. "There's something else I've got to do first." He smiled tiredly.

"Wait for me. Maybe they'll make some coffee in the dining room for us."

She nodded without speaking, and this time as he turned to pass, she did not attempt to detain him.

Now, except for little crowds of curious men here and there along the roadway, the town was quiet again. As the loner stepped down into the roadway slush to push on over to the jailhouse, he saw those little dark clutches of curious people. Afterwards, as he reached for the jailhouse door, he also saw lights coming on here and there. He entered the jailhouse.

Joe Conway was slouching upon the edge of his desk, dourly considering Frank Lester and Lorenzo Simpson. Abel and several others turned as the loner came in out of the bitter night, but no one spoke to him. There was something else going on here that held those men's attention.

Conway said, "Simpson, I want you to draw me a map of where you fellers hid that gold." Joe got up from his desk and made a curt gesture with one hand. "Sit down there and start working."

Simpson shot the loner a quick look, dropped his eyes, and passed over to take the deputy's chair.

Conway removed his hat, flung it aside, and looked over where the loner was standing, beside Abel Poirer.

"They told where the gold's hidden," he said. "They

also admitted it came from those stage holdups down south."

"What about Hennesey?" the loner asked.

Conway nodded his head over this question. "We had it figured about right. Pat was the brains behind all this. Robbin' the stages was to give the bunch of them operatin' capital to work their land scheme. Simpson says Pat meant to bankrupt every cow outfit for fifty miles around by buying up land patents an' resellin' 'em to squatters."

Abel Poirer and his Yellowstone riders looked away from Joe as he made this statement; they fixed their cold looks of raw enmity upon the two survivors of Pat Hennesey's gun crew. The loner saw those looks. He thought that, except for Joe and himself and perhaps Abel, Vern and the other Yellowstone men would have gone to their saddles up at the livery barn, taken down two good hard-twist lariats, and made very short work of Simpson and Frank Lester.

"One more thing," murmured the loner, walking over close to the lawman, "Open your safe, Joe, and give me those land patents you took off Tom Smith."

Without a word, Conway crossed to the safe, hunkered down to work the tumblers, and swung back the door. As he drew forth a thick bundle of papers held together by a dirty little length of string, he said, "One thing puzzles me about these papers: why didn't

Tom Smith or whatever his name was, turn them over to Hennesey right after he hit town?"

Lorenzo Simpson looked up from over at Conway's desk, where he was drawing his map, and said, "He was willin', but Pat had a better idea. Pat said for Tom to keep them patents so's the loner wouldn't think Tom already worked with the rest of us. Pat had the idea that if the loner thought Tom was also a loner—a feller who worked by himself—he just might decide to throw in with Tom. That way, accordin' to Pat, we'd wind up with *all* the patents, and maybe it wouldn't cost us a dime of cash money. Anyway, Pat figured maybe the loner'd throw in with us."

Conway stood up, looking disgruntled. "Shut up and finish that map," he growled at Simpson. He half turned, handed the papers to the loner, blew out a big, ragged breath, and wagged his head back and forth. "Now," he mumbled, "you'll give those papers to Poirer and Yellowstone'll remain intact. I figure that's best. Without Yellowstone, this town'd lose a lot of trade."

But the loner shook his head at Joe, pocketed the papers, and turned away. He got as far as the door before Conway, standing there looking dumbfounded, squawked at him.

"Hey! Where you goin'?"

"For a little walk," replied the loner, twisting to gaze around at all those faces. "See you boys later."

The loner had the door open, was passing through it when Conway squawked at him again. This time, though, the loner didn't face around. He passed on out into the bitter-cold night, and behind him, Abel Poirer threw out a hand when Conway would have rushed after him.

"It's all right," said Poirer. "Let him go, Joe. He's going to do this *his* way."

"Huh? His way?"

"Earlier, you wondered why he and I seemed bitter towards one another. I'll tell you why that was, Joe. My daughter is in love with him. I didn't like that. Not when I first learnt about it, I didn't, but later—after I met my wife and Toni over at the hotel tonight—well—it's her life. I want only what's best for her." Abel looked around at the faces turned towards him. He made a little abashed smile. "You boys understand?" he asked of his Yellowstone riders.

Vern and the others nodded without speaking, but old Puma, true to type, rushed in with words where the others, more circumspect, kept silent. Old Puma said, "I always said you was a real feller, Mister Poirer, only you had your worries too, and Miss Toni—!"

John Landon's concealed elbow dug viciously into old Puma's back on one side. On the other side, youthful Drew Ruddabaugh, while outwardly smiling over at his employer, brought one heavy boot down across old

Puma's half-frozen toes, causing the old cowboy to gasp and grimace and go skipping quickly away from those two.

Out in the quiet night, the loner re-crossed through roadway morass, paused to kick clods of congealing mud from his boots, then walked slowly along towards the hotel. He did not look pleased that all this had come to a satisfactory conclusion. He didn't look happy or even anticipatory as he approached that closed glass door with its twin carriage lamps upon opposite sides.

He entered the lobby, blinked where bright light struck him hard across the face, saw Toni standing over by the stove, saw Nettie Poirer sitting in a large chair looking tired but happy, and removed his hat as he gently nodded to them both.

There was no one else in the lobby, which was odd considering all that had so violently happened so recently. But a closer scrutiny of Nettie Poirer's determined jaw might have explained how the night-clerk and the local loafers had been prevailed upon to leave so that her daughter and the loner might be uninterrupted when he returned to the hotel.

Toni smiled over at him, nodded at a little table where a pot of steaming coffee stood between two sets of cups and saucers, and she moved forward to meet him at that little table.

He went forward feeling the wonderful warmth of

the room. He was tired, and this warmth made him feel that weariness all the more.

He dug out the bundle of land patents Conway had given him, tossed them down as Toni offered him a cup of coffee, and said, "That should do it. Those are the last of the land claims covering all of the Yellowstone range." He took the cup and smiled gently over at Toni. "The other night, when we stood out on your porch watching the snow fall, you said Yellowstone meant everything to you. Well, it probably never would have worked out as Hennesey wanted it to anyway, but whether it might have or not, all those land patents will take care of that now. No one can ever squat legally on Yellowstone land now."

He lifted his cup in a little salute and drank. Over the rim of his cup, he saw dark and moving things in the beautiful eyes across that little table from him. He finished the coffee, carefully set the cup down, and turned towards Nettie Poirer.

"You had reason to dislike me," he said to the older woman. "I was disagreeable when I was laid up at the ranch. I can't expect you to see me as being any different now than I was then. But I'd like to ask one favor of you, Mrs. Poirer. Give me a chance to see your daughter. Give me a chance to be what I used to be."

Nettie got up out of her chair. She had a frilly small handkerchief in one hand, which she put up to her face now, then lowered it to say. "It's the cold. It makes my eyes run." She considered her radiant daughter. She put a long, grave gaze upon the loner.

"Mister—er—Loner. "

"Flynn, ma'am. Cole Flynn."

"Mister Cole Flynn, my daughter is a woman, not a child. She can make her own—"

"No," said the loner, breaking in. "No, ma'am, I want *your* approval."

Nettie brought the little handkerchief up again. She smiled at the loner from eyes brimming with unshed tears.

"You have my permission, Mister Flynn," she said quietly. "Now, if you two will excuse me, it's late, and this has been an ordeal for me. I want to walk over and get Abel."

The loner moved. "I'll get him. It's cold out there, and the roadway is ankle deep in mud."

Nettie threw up a restraining hand. "Mister Flynn," she said sharply. "I've walked through colder nights than this one for my husband in years past. Besides, as you probably know right this minute, there are times when it's much better for people to meet alone."

The loner stood still, watching Nettie adjust her cape. He slowly smiled as she turned and started for the roadside doorway.

Toni came around to stand at his side. He felt her

fingers steal into his hand. He closed his hand tightly around them. They stood shoulder to shoulder like that with the good warmth all around them for a long, tender moment, before the loner turned, reached out, and she came eagerly into his arms.

ABOUT THE AUTHOR

Lauran Paine was born in Duluth, Minnesota, a descendant of the Revolutionary War patriot and author, Thomas Paine. His family moved to California where he spent years in the livestock trade and rodeos, and where he learned from many old-timers how different the Old West was from the way movies portrayed it. After serving in the Navy in World War II, he began writing for Western pulp magazines. By 1948, he was writing full-time. He wrote more than a thousand books under his own name and pseudonyms, including hundreds of Westerns as well as romance, science fiction, and mystery novels. His books were adapted twice into films: *Law Man* as the 1957 movie *The Quiet Gun*, and the novel originally titled *The Open Range Men* as 2003's *Open Range*, with Kevin Costner, Robert Duval, and Annette Benning.